THAT SUMMER WE STOLE OUR PERMANENT RECORDS

D0885459

ALSO BY KERSTI NIEBRUEGGE

The Zonderling

A young Midwestern woman moves into The Zonderling, a cheap, old-fashioned residential hotel that has been home to the fair young ladies of New York City (no men allowed!) since 1905.

"A hilariously funny, compact volume about a hotel's denizens that delivers well-aimed zingers—a winner."

— *Kirkus Reviews*

Mistake, Wisconsin

Deep in Wisconsin's eccentric Northwoods, a high school sophomore realizes she must take on a corrupt politician if she wants to save her town's beloved holiday—musky fishing Opening Day.

"Debut author Niebruegge creates a light, humorous mystery filled with Midwestern references—cheese curds, lutefisk dinners, supper clubs, and high school sports—and a touch of Northwoods folklore."

— *Publishers Weekly*

"*Mistake, Wisconsin* is a deftly crafted Wisconsin culture based novel that demonstrates author Kersti Niebruegge's impressive storytelling talents ideal for young adult readers."

— *Midwest Book Review*

THAT SUMMER WE STOLE OUR PERMANENT RECORDS

Kersti Niebruegge

▼▲▼▲▼

Kersti Niebruegge
Milwaukee

Cover design by Kersti Niebruegge.
Artwork and photo by Kersti Niebruegge.

ISBN (paperback): 978-0-9908710-9-5
ISBN (Kindle eBook): 978-0-9908710-8-8
ISBN (EPUB eBook): 978-0-9908710-5-7

Library of Congress Control Number: 2018911916

For everyone who is always nice to the New Kid.
(Which is totally, most definitely all of you, right? *Right?!*)

CONTENTS

▼ ▲ ▼ ▲ ▼

COHEN, Candice

DULLES, Becky

JUNEAU, Johnny

LEE, Gina

MCNUTT, Bobby

MCNUTT, Tommy

RODRIGUEZ, Diana

That Summer
We Stole Our
Permanent Records

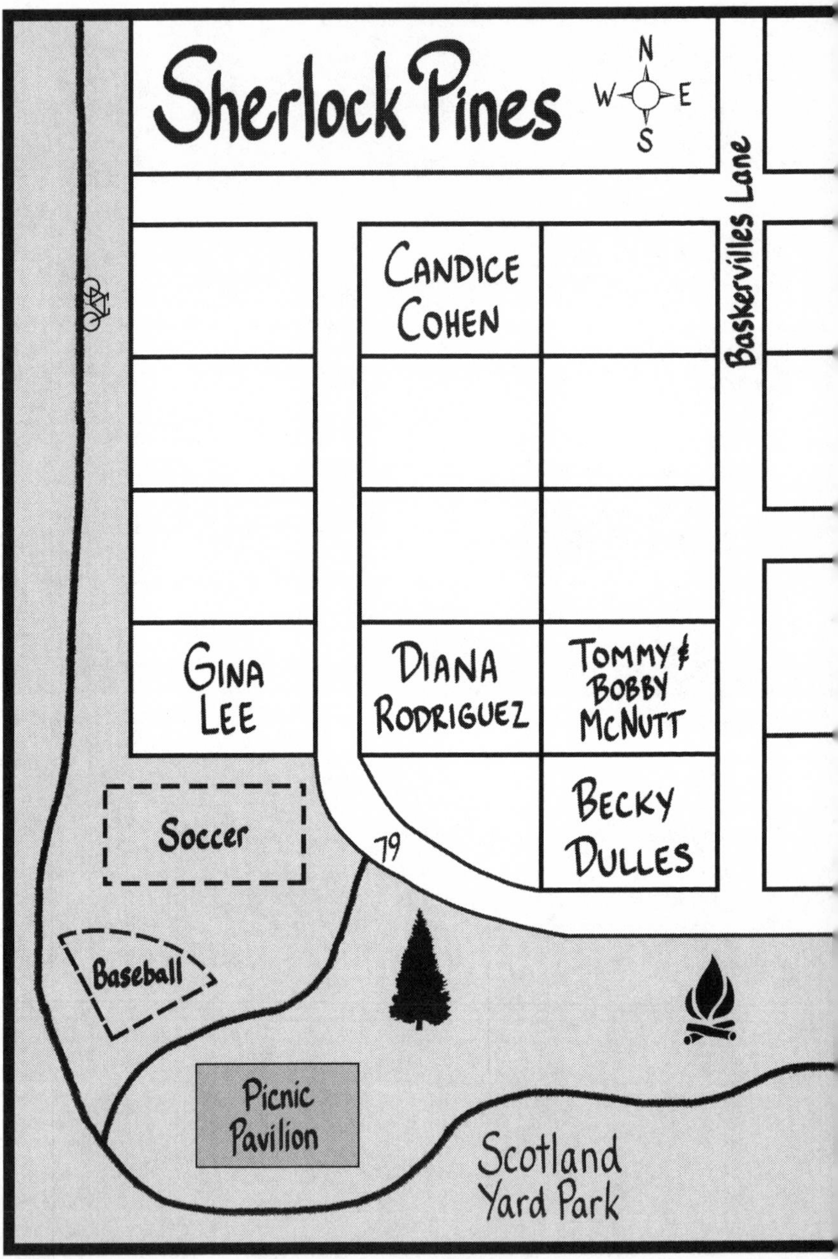
Sherlock Pines
N
W
E
S
Baskervilles Lane
Candice Cohen
Gina Lee
Diana Rodriguez
Tommy & Bobby McNutt
Becky Dulles
Soccer
79
Baseball
Picnic Pavilion
Scotland Yard Park

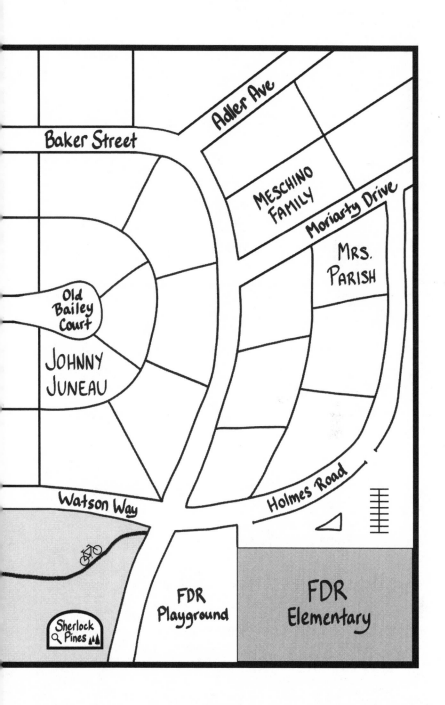

CHAPTER ONE

Worst. News. Ever.

▼ ▲ ▼ ▲ ▼

When the school year wrapped up in 1993, I was itching to return the following fall as the biggest Big Kid of them all. Yes, after summer vacation, I, Becky Dulles, was finally going to be a sixth grader at Franklin D. Roosevelt Elementary, with all the perks and benefits I'd been waiting for!

Daydreaming about sixth grade had become my new favorite pastime (second only to collecting Canadian coins and hummingbird magnets). However, something even better filled my mind during the assembly on Friday, May 21—the mouthwatering scent of restaurant pizza. Not delivery pizza. Not frozen pizza. But real restaurant pizza.

From Viv's Pizza Place!

The special lunch was part of FDR's end-of-year festivities, and I impatiently waited for the principal, Mrs. Parish, to finish babbling so I could dig into the gooey cheese.

Blah, blah, blah, "1992 to 1993 was a wonderful school year," she said. Blah, blah, blah, "school district." Blah, blah, blah, "budget."

I was starving and bored out of my mind while sitting on the shiny gym floor with five hundred students. At least my best friends—the Sherlock Pines Gang—surrounded me: Diana Rodriguez, Candice Cohen, Gina Lee, Johnny Juneau, and the McNutt twins, Tommy and Bobby. The seven of us had known each other nearly all our lives, and we lived within a three-house radius in Sherlock Pines, a subdivision where everything was named after stuff from Sherlock Holmes stories.

After we had listened to the principal drone on for what felt like one thousand hours, Gina turned to me in a panic. "The mozzarella is getting all cold and ruined!"

"Ugh, I know! She keeps going on and on about nothing just to torture us."

Diana groaned and twisted her brunette half-up side ponytail. "I sure hope Mrs. Parish ordered enough pepperoni this time."

Gina and I nodded. A riot nearly broke out last year when everyone discovered that most of the pizzas were covered in vegetables. Vegetables! Ruining restaurant pizza with vegetables was such an outrageous violation of the Law of Kids that I wrote a letter to my local councilwoman to complain. She responded and told me that she understood my concerns, but vegetables could be pretty tasty on pizza if I gave them a chance.

I had never been more disappointed in an elected official.

My mind desperately needed to focus on something besides the potential pepperoni crisis. I began readjusting the barrette that held back my awkward auburn bangs. (They were growing out after a horrible haircut at my grandma's so-called beauty shop.) As I fixed my bobbed hair, I stared at the dragons that Johnny was drawing on his sneakers. He and the McNutts were sitting two rows in front of me, and they kept turning around to make sure the pizza hadn't disappeared into the mouths of the teachers keeping guard.

Johnny noticed me staring at his shoes, and he waved to catch my eye. "Becky," he whispered, "my sister gave me her old walkie-talkies."

At last! The Sherlock Pines Gang finally had a secret-communications device that was fancier than leaving notes in the tree hollow in Scotland Yard Park.

I smiled and gave Johnny a thumbs-up. "Let's test them soon!"

"Test what?" Tommy asked.

"The walkie-talkies from Jenny," Johnny answered.

"Cool! We can use them on that stakeout I have planned to see what's digging a hole in my bucket of dirt!" Bobby said, high-fiving his brother.

The McNutts were identical twins, but Bobby had seven freckles that looked like the Big Dipper on his left cheek. Those little marks had been mighty helpful to FDR teachers in determining which blond McNutt had sprayed them with Zany Ribbons–brand party string, as the boys often did whenever there was a sale at Delta Sue's Dime Store. It was too bad there hadn't been a recent sale at Delta Sue's because a little Zany Ribbons would have made Mrs. Parish's speech a lot more interesting.

Just as I was wishing for something exciting to happen, a handful of kids gasped. The sharp intake of breath was isolated among those who were sitting closest to Mrs. Parish (and those farthest from the distracting pizza aroma). No one around me knew what the principal had said, but a quiet murmur began filtering through the crowd.

Candice glanced up from painting her nails with white correction fluid. "What's going on? Did her slip fall down again?" Despite jerking around to get a better view, Candice's short light-brown hair stayed in stylish formation, thanks to a heavy coat of hairspray.

"I know this is upsetting, but we will make it as easy as possible," Mrs. Parish said.

The quiet murmur spiked to a medium-high murmur as everyone tried to figure out what scary thing the principal was going to make easy. I hoped it didn't involve mandatory attendance at the annual cleaning day, an event where Mrs. Parish served another round of restaurant pizza to lure kid volunteers back to FDR. Even with the tempting offer, I'd never helped. The only kids who were crazy enough to spend the first day of summer vacation at school were the brownnosers.

Brownnosers like Tricia Meschino.

She was sitting behind me in the gym, and I accidentally made eye contact with her while trying to understand what was happening.

Delighted, as always, to be a thorn in my side, Tricia smirked at me. "We're all getting sent to new schools next year."

"Stop making up rumors again," I said, irritated.

"I'm not lying, dummy. Listen!" She motioned for me to look at Mrs. Parish.

By this point the medium-high murmur had turned into a full-on roar that consumed the room. A small amount of panic started bubbling inside the hungry, growling pit of my stomach.

"Settle down," the principal said. "Remember you're at an assembly. You should be listening and at voice-level zero."

"Then tell us what's going on around here, Mrs. Parish!" I yelled.

I was not alone in my exasperation. A chorus of hungry voices agreed and chanted, "Tell us! Tell us! Tell us!"

"I'm waiting for voice-level zero."

We got quiet lickety-split. No one wanted to risk losing restaurant pizza because of a voice-level violation, especially when there was some sort of disaster looming on the horizon.

"As I was saying," Mrs. Parish continued, "due to last-minute budget cuts, Franklin D. Roosevelt is closing this summer."

Kaboom!

All of us sat in stunned silence, too shocked to react to the insane words coming out of the principal's mouth. Three long seconds ticked by before the whole room erupted in protests that echoed off the cinder block walls. There was no time to worry about voice levels and restaurant pizza—not when we had to stop the closure of the best school in the country!

One boy said he was going to call the governor!

One girl said she was going to call the president!

Another girl said she was going to call Michael Keaton because Batman could most definitely stop Mrs. Parish's evil ways!

The principal signaled for us to calm down. "I'm sorry but there isn't enough money in the budget to keep the school open, no matter who you're going to call."

"Ghost-bust-ers!" the McNutts shouted with glee.

"That didn't sound like voice-level zero," Mrs. Parish cautioned. "Look, I understand how difficult it is to leave FDR and attend different schools in the fall."

I had to leave FDR?

I had to leave FDR!

The world had gone topsy-turvy!

I had to be a Big Kid sixth grader at . . . where did I have to go? For the love of pizza, where did I have to go?

"With the redistricting, half of you will go to Lenah Higbee Elementary and half will go to Meadow View," Mrs. Parish said.

"Meadow View?" Candice said, appalled. "Their playground doesn't have monkey bars."

"And Lenah Higbee doesn't have hopscotch," Gina said.

"But that's gotta be against the law!" I said.

"That's not even the worst thing," Diana said. "Neither school takes kids on a camping trip for sixth-grade graduation."

"*What?* We're losing our camping trip?" I looked around for hidden cameras, hoping the whole announcement had been some stupid, terrible practical joke. But I only saw a ton of worried kids.

It was real. I really had to leave FDR!

"You will attend Lenah Higbee if you live on Baskervilles Lane or east of Baskervilles Lane," Mrs. Parish said. "Everyone west of Baskervilles Lane will go to Meadow View."

I frantically turned to my friends. "Where's east?"

"Australia is near the Far East," Gina said, furrowing her brow as she thought out loud. "And you get to Australia by digging a deep hole, which means we don't live east 'cause none of us live that way."

Bewildered, I watched her gesture to the floor. "What are you talking about? This is not the time for more of your Australia facts, Gina!" Jeez Louise, she'd been obsessed with that place ever since she saw the new koalas at the zoo.

"Yeah, Gina, you're not making any sense," Candice said. "Everyone knows you go to *China* if you dig a deep hole."

Gina shook her head so forcefully that the scrunchie on her french braid smacked her face. "You go to Australia. That's why it's called Down Under. Because it's on the direct opposite side of the planet from us."

Candice reached into her pocket. "I'll bet you a dime! Ask anyone in here where you go if you—"

"No one cares about digging holes!" I snapped. "Mrs. Parish said everyone on Baskervilles and everyone east of Baskervilles goes to Lenah Higbee."

"And everyone the other way is Meadow View," Diana said. She slowly looked at Candice and Gina. "That means . . . we're Meadow View."

I scowled. "We get no monkey bars."

"Except you," Diana said. "You live *on* Baskervilles."

The ghastly fact hung over me like a creepy vampire bat. "I don't want to spend a year at Lenah Higbee with just Johnny and the McNutts!"

Gina gasped. "But it's not just a year. Lenah Higbee kids go to a different middle school. And they don't go to Susan B. Anthony High School. They go to—"

"*Central High.*" My heart broke as the catastrophic news sunk in. I'd been put on a different track for high school! Gina, Diana, and Candice were still going to Susan B. Anthony, but Mrs. Parish was shipping me and the boys off to Central High. I was not going to graduate with the whole Sherlock Pines Gang!

Nearly in tears, I distracted myself by playing with my glow-in-the-dark sneakers. As I flicked the hot-pink laces, I realized Mrs. Parish was still yakking away about the tragedy.

"Just because school is closing does not mean you have an excuse to fool around," she warned. "No stealing kickballs, art supplies, the cuckoo clock photo, nothing. And no writing on your desks or the bathroom walls. If I catch you doing anything like that, what happens?"

In weary unison, every kid replied, "It goes on our permanent record."

"And your permanent records are?"

"Permanent."

We knew this routine in our sleep because we'd probably answered the same questions from Mrs. Parish about one zillion times.

"Correct. Permanent records always stay with you. They're all boxed up in the teachers' lounge, waiting to go to your new schools. But I assure you I will dig out your file and add anything that needs to be added if I catch you being naughty."

My jaw dropped. *Permanent records?* Right then and there, my sadness morphed into anger. Wild-eyed, I turned to my friends. "How can Mrs. Parish threaten us with permanent records at a time like this?"

"Because it always works," Diana said.

It was true. After the principal made her threat, the entire student body moved rapidly from voice-level bazillion to voice-level one. The reaction would have been the same anywhere in America because every kid shared a hatred of the most frightening thing at school: the permanent record.

Sure, grown-ups claimed that permanent records contained nothing more than report cards and attendance information. They insisted that those paper files were harmless progress summaries handed to each student's new teacher every year until high school graduation.

But I knew that was a bunch of baloney.

In fact, all kids knew that was a bunch of baloney! Because if that claim were true, it didn't make sense why so many teachers and principals threatened to write a permanent-record update anytime any kid did anything kinda, sorta, maybe naughty. Exhibit A: exactly what Mrs. Parish did one minute ago.

"It's all so unfair," I said. "FDR closing and us getting split up and—"

"Permanent records going to new schools," Diana chimed in.

"Meadow View not having monkey bars," Candice added.

"And cheese getting cold on restaurant pizza," Gina grumbled while twirling the loose black hair at the end of her braid.

I intensely drummed my fingers on my knees. "We can't let Mrs. Parish do this to us."

Stopping the principal would be a nearly impossible task, especially since I was just a kid and she was an adult literally licensed by the state to ruin kids' lives. Even so, I was bound and determined to throw a wrench into the works.

But first things first—there was a slice of pepperoni with my name on it, and I joined the stampede the second that the McNutts screamed, "Pizza time!"

CHAPTER TWO

This Is Going on Your Permanent Record

▼ ▲ ▼ ▲ ▼

Many of the most historic disputes in the world had been resolved with a game of rock-paper-scissors. And that Saturday night at Candice's house, Gina and I had a serious situation to settle.

"One, two, three!" we chanted.

Smiling, Gina smashed my fingers with her fist. "Rock crushes scissors!"

"Two out of three," I pleaded.

"Nope! Mark-Paul Gosselaar is mine!" Gina grabbed the new issue of *Duende Teen*, a fashion and celebrity magazine, and cut out a full-page photo of the teen dreamboat, who played Zack Morris on *Saved by the Bell*.

Both of us wanted to tape Mark-Paul's picture inside our desks at school, and I was so mad at myself for being the chump who changed from paper to scissors at the last second.

"I'm next!" Diana snatched the magazine from Gina and paged through it until she got to a rare two-page photo spread. "Hello, Brad Pitt!"

"Brad Pitt!" I said with mock horror. "What would Curtis say?"

Diana's crush on Gina's fourteen-year-old brother started two weeks ago when she saw him skateboarding on a homemade ramp in his driveway. I didn't understand the appeal of that lunkhead, an eighth grader who had purposely knocked a plate out of my hand at last year's block party, but Diana was smitten.

"He'd say, 'Diana, forget about that fly-fishing dude! Please go to the dance with me!' And I'd say, 'Brad who? Of course I'll go to the dance with you!'"

"No, Curtis would say, 'Gina, get your butt outta here 'cause Will and I need to watch *The Wizard of Oz* so we can write our book reports,'" Gina whined. "Now I'll never get those life-changing make-up tips from Oprah."

"Cheer up—his teacher will know he cheated when he writes about Dorothy's red shoes," Candice said as she stuffed popcorn into her mouth. "She wears silver shoes in the book."

Gina happily cackled like the Wicked Witch of the West. "You're gonna get an F, Curtis!"

"What do you think will happen to the school library books when FDR closes?" I asked.

Candice's face lit up. "We should take some home! Mrs. Parish would never know. She'd think they lost the books while closing up."

"No way!" I said. "She'll know, and she'll add it to your permanent record."

"Already boxed up for the new schools," Gina said, while sucking on a cherry-flavored Fruity Bijou, a ring-shaped candy she'd just put on her finger.

"So what? If a new school cared about an old school's permanent record, then Mrs. Parish would have mentioned it when I moved here," Candice said.

As the only kid I knew who had lived in a different state, Candice was really interesting. She moved to Sherlock Pines the summer before fourth grade, and she used all sorts of bizarre words for things. For example, Candice said the word *pop* when she was talking about soda, and she used the word *highways* when she was talking about freeways. She also had a weird way of pronouncing *caramel* that made no sense whatsoever. But at the same time, Candice thought it was completely wacky that her new neighborhood was named after a fictional detective.

Even though she thought our words for streets and candy were odd, Candice instantly became part of the Sherlock Pines Gang after introducing us to her dog, Daisy, and Daisy's three puppies named Huey, Dewey, and Louie. There were a lot of after-school trips to Candice's house to play with the world's cutest Pomeranians, who were all currently trying to steal snacks off the coffee table.

Diana reached over Louie's hopeful face and dipped a chip into some salsa. "What kind of stuff is in your file from your old school?"

"I dunno. Normal things," Candice said, brushing popcorn crumbs off her floral-print vest. "Like all the times the principal caught me stealing school chalk."

Gina yanked the Fruity Bijou out of her mouth. "That went on your permanent record?" She pulled two pieces of chalk from her pocket. "I took these from Mr. Khan yesterday!"

I shrugged. "Everyone steals school chalk."

It was true. School chalk was a thousand times better than the powdery junk sold at Delta Sue's Dime Store, so it was a prized item to swipe for home chalkboards. I'd pocketed a whole box of the good stuff when Mrs. Parish made me clean erasers as a punishment during third grade.

But Gina was still worried. "I've been taking school chalk since I was seven."

"You've never been caught, though," Diana said reassuringly. "You'd know if you had a bunch of scary stuff in your file. Mrs. Parish would have called you down and told you all about it."

"Like the McNutts," I said. "They were in her office all afternoon yesterday because they stole some kickballs."

"You're right," Gina said. "I gotta take a chill pill."

Candice finished a long drink from a chocolate milkshake and then dramatically yanked the straw out of her mouth. "But what if she doesn't?"

Gina quickly became defensive. "Maybe *you* need to take a chill pill!"

"Not you—Mrs. Parish. What if she writes secret updates to permanent records? Why should we trust that she's telling us the truth about everything?"

Terror washed over Gina's face. "I'm screwed. We're all screwed!"

"Candice is right! It's so obvious now that I think about it," Diana said. "My old babysitter once told me that her sister's friend's brother was banned from Disney World because of something in his permanent record."

"No!" Gina wailed. "I've never even been to Florida yet!"

"I bet this is why the water park bans kids for no reason," I said.

"And bosses at jobs can see your permanent record too," Diana added. "What if I never get to work at the Supreme Court just because Mrs. Parish made up some crazy thing about me when I was eight?"

I was disgusted. "Permanent record time bombs . . . waiting for all of us."

"Wait's over, girls! Get 'em while they're hot!" Mrs. Cohen announced as she entered the family room with a platter of burgers and fries. "Anything else you need for your party?"

"Gimme the remote, Mom," Candice said. "The *Saved by the Bell* finale starts in one minute."

Diana, Gina, Candice, and I had planned a sleepover ever since we'd found out the tragic news that our favorite TV show was ending. *Saved by the Bell* taught us everything we thought we needed to know for when we started high school—like how important it is to be friends forever, to win the annual prank war, and to never let an oil company drill near the football field.

It was going to be tough watching our favorite pretend friends—high school seniors Kelly, Zack, Slater, Jessie, Lisa, and Screech—say farewell to each other and their beloved Bayside High. Especially when I knew that I'd never have the same graduation experience with all my best friends.

Sheesh! Between *Saved by the Bell* and FDR, the number of monumental goodbyes I was going to have to make in May of 1993 was really stacking up.

▲ ▼ ▲

When Candice and I arrived in class on Monday, our teacher was slouched in her chair, loudly slurping coffee. I waved a sympathetic hello to Mrs. Andrews, who I assumed was super upset about saying goodbye to FDR too. Suddenly, the principal burst through the door and marched Johnny, Bobby, and Tommy into the room.

The McNutts versus Mrs. Parish had been amazing entertainment since 1987, so my classmates and I immediately devoted our attention to the face-off. It was too bad that Gina and Diana would miss the show just because they were stuck next door in Mr. Khan's class. On the other hand, they were currently gazing at FDR's youngest and cutest teacher, while I was racing to my seat, trying to steer clear of the principal's evil eye.

"Yes, Tommy," Mrs. Parish said as she herded the boys through a maze of desks. "You've told me many times that your mom is a lawyer."

"And she'll tell you that we can fry ants if we want to—it's a free country!"

"But that doesn't mean you can start a fire."

Bobby threw his hands up in the air. "Like I said, we can't help it if some leaves happen to blow directly under our magnifying glasses and stay there until they catch fire."

"I didn't fry anything, Mrs. Parish," Johnny argued. "I wasn't even sitting on the ground yet."

The principal held up three magnifying glasses. "Then why were you holding one of these?"

"Since when is it a crime to hold a magnifying glass?"

"Uh oh!" Bobby jokingly pointed to Mrs. Parish. "We caught you red-handed!"

"Case closed!" Tommy said. "Guilty as charged! Order in the—"

"Sit down. This is going on your permanent record."

Whoa! Straight to the big guns of school discipline! I was on the edge of my seat.

"That is so unfair, Mrs. Parish! I didn't do anything, and now you're going to write that I did and send it to my new school," Johnny protested. "Why don't you ever give anyone a break?"

"Because she's a sadist," Tommy said.

I didn't know the meaning of the word *sadist*, and I knew that Tommy didn't either. But he told me that his mom used the term to describe her dentist after she returned from a painful appointment, so Tommy knew it wasn't a nice thing to call someone. Judging by the principal's reaction, I knew he was right.

"Sit. Down. *Now,*" Mrs. Parish growled.

Johnny slumped into the desk next to mine, but the McNutts were totally unfazed by another entry in their files. With a rap sheet of farting contests, switching identities, and slicing open beanbag chairs in the library (to verify type of bean), the McNutts' permanent records had been updated as many times as a ranking of the best bubble gum flavors.

Sometimes the McNutts were so weird that they *wanted* to go to the principal's office. Like last Friday when they purposely stole four kickballs in front of Mrs. Parish, right after the assembly where she told us not to take anything. Just as the McNutts had planned, she dragged them to her office and left them alone while she fetched their permanent records from the moving boxes. With Mrs. Parish out of sight, the twins moved a lamp and wrote a sneaky message on her desk: "Bobby McNutt & Tommy McNutt were here . . . a lot. 1993 rules!"

But the principal apparently had no time to haul anyone to her office for a talking-to about the playground fire. As the bell rang, Mrs. Parish handed the magnifying glasses to my teacher and said, "Give these back at the end of the day." Next she sized up Mrs. Andrews's rumpled appearance and red eyes. "Are you OK?"

"I was out—I mean up! Um . . ."

At that very moment, Candice sneezed multiple times, one right after the other.

"Allergies!" Mrs. Andrews said hurriedly. "I was up because of allergies. Didn't sleep all night."

Satisfied with the explanation, the principal turned to leave. When she got to the doorway, she wheeled around and scanned the room like a hawk hunting for prey. Every kid, even tattletale Tricia Meschino, avoided eye contact in case Mrs. Parish was searching for another file-update victim.

"If I catch anyone else burning anything, regardless of whether you are using matches or a magnifying glass, it is going on your permanent record. Understood?"

We replied like a bunch of robots. "Yes, Mrs. Parish."

"Good. Have a happy Monday, everybody."

And with that dumb goodbye, classroom 501 was finally free of the principal and her rotten threats.

Mrs. Andrews finished glugging from the coffee mug she bought during her recent honeymoon and slowly stood up. "OK, guys, all this talking and fluorescent light is giving me a headache."

"Maybe you should go to the nurse," I said. The suggestion was extremely popular with my classmates, who encouraged our teacher to leave us alone for as long as she needed until she felt better.

"I'm fine," Mrs. Andrews said, walking toward the light switch by the door. "I was just up late at a wedding. And Tommy," she added with a smirk, "if you want to know what a real sadist is, it's people who have Sunday weddings."

"Ha ha, good one, Mrs. Andrews!" Tommy said, comically slapping his knee. "Sunday weddings!"

I didn't understand what was so funny, but Tommy sure made a show of laughing at Mrs. Andrews's joke. I assumed he was trying to rack up end-of-year brownie points, since I had no idea why people like Mrs. Parish or dentists would host Sunday weddings. And I was definitely smarter than the McNutts, two boys who frequently attacked each other with water balloons because they forgot to tell the other one about a stakeout they were doing.

After switching the lights off, Mrs. Andrews sighed in relief. "Much better."

"You're like my dad last Friday morning," Candice said. "He didn't want to see any lights after he went to a party at Roberta's Tavern to watch the *Cheers* finale. Did you throw up too?"

The McNutts, who never missed a good puke reference, made some top-notch retching noises as they doubled over in their chairs.

Ignoring both the McNutts' theatrics and Candice's question, Mrs. Andrews asked us for a favor. "For the rest of the morning, we're going to be real quiet and watch movies before lunch. Sound good?"

Seeing as no kid in the history of the world had ever objected to watching a video, any video, at school, I nodded enthusiastically along with everybody else.

Mrs. Andrews picked up the phone that was hanging under the mounted television and called the school librarian. She had a short discussion with Mr. Lockett about the quietest videotapes that he could play for us, then she turned on the TV and flipped to channel three. "We're watching something about Earth Day followed by something about Apollo 11. Everyone think about saving the environment and becoming astronauts."

Having dispensed those ambitious instructions, Mrs. Andrews returned to her desk, put her head down, and closed her eyes.

I dutifully turned my attention to the Earth Day program, which I'd already seen twice on PBS.

Tommy made the first move one minute later when he started playing video poker on a handheld toy. The rest of us patiently waited to see whether Mrs. Andrews would notice the beeping game over the noisy humpback whales on the TV screen.

Bobby's eyes darted back and forth from Tommy to our teacher as he assessed the situation. An excruciating eleven seconds ticked by before he made the call: "All clear!"

Activity burst to life at each four-desk pod as everyone stopped pretending to watch TV. I lifted the photo-covered (but sadly Mark-Paul Gosselaar–free) lid on my desk and took out some markers and loose-leaf paper. Very carefully, I started folding the paper to make a cootie catcher (or as Candice called it, a paper origami fortune-teller) to play with during recess.

We were all enjoying a leisurely Monday morning, so naturally Tricia Meschino tried to ruin it.

She raised her hand and shouted, "Mrs. Andrews! No one is watching the video."

Everyone froze except for Johnny. He continued doodling dragons in his assignment notebook with markers that I'd loaned him.

Barely moving, Mrs. Andrews mumbled, "It's fine, Tricia."

Without missing a beat, Bobby launched a paper airplane at Tricia and watched it smash into her curled, blonde hair. He made a face at her and resumed carving his name into his desk with a pair of compasses. (Like any kid seeking eternal glory, Bobby and his brother were determined to leave their mark on FDR in as many spots as possible before it closed.)

Tricia tucked a dislodged strand of long hair back under her velvet headband. "Mrs. Andrews," she whined. "Bobby hit me with a paper airplane!"

"Tricia, please! No more talking."

"But, Bobby—"

"Is anything on fire?"

"No, but—"

"Then I don't want to hear about it."

Mad as a swarm of yellow jackets, Tricia picked up the paper airplane and threw it at Bobby. But it plummeted to the floor, the impact squashing the nose of the plane. Bobby promptly fell out of his chair so he could roll in the aisle with laughter.

I chuckled while watching his over-the-top antics. It was always satisfying to see a meanie like Tricia Meschino get what she deserved.

She whipped around and glared at me. "What are you laughing at, Dull Becky Dulles?"

Dull Becky Dulles. That had been the go-to insult ever since Tricia thought she struck nickname gold in kindergarten. I plucked the bent, misshapen airplane off the floor and held it up. "Even wide-ruled paper doesn't wanna play with tattletales."

"Oh, Dull Becky Dulles thinks she's funny," Tricia snapped. "It crashed because Bobby didn't fold it right!"

Giggles began rolling through the classroom as the Meschino meltdown became more and more entertaining.

In response, Tricia coolly opened her lunch bag and removed a king-size chocolate bar. She held it high above her head, making as much noise as possible with her bangle bracelets. Once Tricia was sure that everyone had seen the treat, she enticingly peeled off the wrapper.

Having a king-size candy bar can make any kid instantly popular. And with sharable chocolate in sight, a bunch of suck-ups stopped laughing at Tricia's tantrum and surrounded her to praise everything she was wearing from her high-tops to her color-changing T-shirt.

But there was no king-size candy bar in the world that could persuade me or anyone else in the Sherlock Pines Gang to suck up to a Meschino—which is why a crisp paper airplane, decorated with dragons, hit Tricia square in the face.

CHAPTER THREE

Becky Gets an Excellent Idea

▼ ▲ ▼ ▲ ▼

"Come in, Johnny! Over," I said into a purple walkie-talkie that was covered with stickers. "Hello? Can you hear me now?"

"Roger! I'm by the tree hollow," Johnny's voice screamed in reply. "Meet you on the seventy-nine. Over and out."

I was already standing on the faded *79* mark that was written on Watson Way in tar. It was the main meeting spot for the Sherlock Pines Gang since it was located halfway between all our homes. The square-foot black number was also the origin of a really cool high school prank.

Drawn long ago by someone in the class of 1979, the landmark had inspired future groups of seniors to paint their own graduation year on roads in the neighborhood. (Someone's dad was always tarring the driveway in May, so a bucket of goo was easy to steal.) I thought the annual tradition was awesome, but my boring parents thought it was vandalism. An opinion that made no sense to me because the tar was on the street, and the street didn't belong to anyone except whoever was playing on it at any given moment.

Like how Watson Way was currently mine.

As I waited for Johnny, I mindlessly kicked at grass clippings in the gutter. The fresh-cut scent got me wondering what Sherlock Pines smelled like back in the olden days when the whole place was farmland. It was crazy to imagine that everything around me used to be corn as far as the eye could see. And all owned by one person: Declan Doyle.

I learned about him in third grade when I had to do a class presentation about local history. He owned not only the biggest farm in town but the most popular dance hall as well (comanaged with his brother-in-law, Lucky Killarney). Declan eventually sold the whole caboodle to developers, and they turned it into Sherlock Pines during the 1960s.

Pretty much everything on the property was demolished to build the subdivision, except for the run-down dance hall. That was remodeled into the Scotland Yard Park picnic pavilion, complete with a big patio, lots of sliding doors, and, to top it all off, a life-size painting of Sherlock Holmes that hung next to the old stone fireplace. The spruced-up building soon became the hub for the neighborhood's most important events—for example, my seventh birthday party.

It was a big Sherlock-themed celebration because I wanted to wear a goofy hat and solve cases just like the famous sleuth and his sidekick, Dr. Watson. I especially wanted to hunt for clues, so my parents created an elaborate detective game and scattered pretend evidence all over Scotland Yard. Using the magnifying glasses that I'd handed out as party favors, my friends and I spent the afternoon dusting for fingerprints by pouring cornstarch on everything lying around. (Something that Johnny's dad did not appreciate when he woke up from his nap in a lawn chair and couldn't see through his sunglasses.)

From that day on, we called ourselves the Sherlock Pines Gang. And the only new member we had ever admitted was Candice.

Just then I saw a founding member emerge from the woods of Scotland Yard, and I stopped fooling around with the grass clippings to wave Johnny over. His wavy brown hair flopped in the breeze as he sprinted to the 79.

"The walkie-talkies are a bust inside the picnic pavilion," Johnny said out of breath. He held up a pair of black plastic glasses with red-and-white swirls on the lenses. "But I found these in the tree hollow."

"Those are Diana's X-ray glasses."

"Do they work?" Johnny asked as he put them on.

"Not yet."

Much to Diana's disappointment, the glasses were a flop when she and I tested them last weekend after playing our first summer parks-and-recreation soccer game. But we knew it had to be illegal for Otter's Joke Shop to sell X-ray glasses if they didn't work, and Diana was determined to figure out how to fix them. In the meantime, she decided to leave the prized specs in the tree hollow so they'd be easy to grab the next time she saw Curtis playing baseball in Scotland Yard.

Despite the failed test run, I was not taking any chances with Johnny wearing X-ray glasses, and I lunged forward to grab them from his face.

"If they're broken, what are you worried about?" he said, ducking out of reach. Then he obnoxiously whistled at me. "Becky!"

"They're not yours!" I said, chasing Johnny in a circle around the *79*.

"Well, they're not yours either."

"Give them to me!"

"Or what?"

"Or . . . or I'll smash your walkie-talkie on the road!" I raised my arm, ready to throw.

"No!" Johnny ripped off the glasses. "No, no, no! Give it to me. Becky, please! Come on!"

"Glasses first."

"Here! Take 'em!" he said, shoving the pair into my hand.

I put the X-ray glasses on my head like a headband, then surrendered the walkie-talkie. I was super relieved because I definitely didn't want to destroy the new secret-communications device.

With the hair-raising showdown over, Johnny and I began walking along Watson Way to go home.

"Are you going anywhere fun this summer?" he asked.

"Only the trips when we all go to P. Tonnes," I said.

"P. Tonnes!"

In a few weeks, the Sherlock Pines Gang was going on the first of several day trips to the best water park in the world: Percival Tonnes Water Park. The Law of Kids required abbreviating the name to P. Tonnes when discussing anything to do with the place. Any kid who didn't make pee jokes by calling it P. Tonnes was immediately assumed to be a snitch for a nosy parent.

Johnny grinned. "When are you going to P. Tonnes?"

"We're all going to P. Tonnes," I said.

"I'm going to P. Tonnes?"

"You're going to P. Tonnes next month."

"Am I going to P. Tonnes with you?"

"Yep! I'm going to P. Tonnes. You're going to P. Tonnes. We're all going to P. Tonnes!"

This hilarious game of wordplay was given to us lucky kids last summer when the Tri-County Water Park was renamed in memory of a guy named Percival Tonnes. Old Percival had never been to a water park in his life and, in fact, hated swimming. But he wanted his name carved into something when he croaked, so he left a bunch of money to the place in his will. The water park was more than happy to accept a large donation and change its name, and tri-county kids were more than happy to joke about the new name.

"These will be our last trips to P. Tonnes before we're shipped off to different schools," I said as we wandered into my backyard. "We were finally going to be the Big Kids at FDR, and now we have to be the New Kids at new schools."

"I've never been the New Kid," Johnny said somberly.

"We have to bring candy like Candice did. It's the only way to survive."

Candice was the sole member of the Sherlock Pines Gang who had ever suffered the trauma of such a terrible situation. But she'd used her brains and quickly erased the dreaded New Kid label by handing out a ton of Fullalove Confectioners candy during her first week at FDR.

Fullalove was a local candy manufacturer that had been around since 1921. Their most popular sweets included Knee-Slapper chocolate bars, Flimflams bite-size fruity candies, and Fruity Bijou candy rings. The company recently expanded into breakfast foods with a delicious toaster pastry named Hullabaloo, which came in a bunch of kid-approved flavors such as Backyard Luau and Surprise Party. As long as I saved enough allowance money to buy a ton of Fullalove goodies, I'd have an OK chance as the New Kid.

"This whole thing stinks," Johnny said. "I'm glad you, me, Tommy, and Bobby are going to the same school, though."

"Even high school?" I asked. "You want to be a Central High *Papermaker?*"

I'd always thought the Papermakers was the lamest team name on the planet, especially when I grew up thinking I was going to be an awesome Falcon at Susan B. Anthony. The loony Papermakers name might have been acceptable in the dark ages when Central High was founded and everyone worked at the paper mill, but it was not a cool name when we were all about to be speeding down the information superhighway thingy.

"Of course I don't want to be a dorky Papermaker. I'm just happy that you and the McNutts will be there to suffer with me," Johnny said. He turned in the direction of FDR and hollered, "Thanks for nothing, Mrs. Parish!"

I covered my ears with my hands. "La la la! Don't say that name!"

Johnny's face lit up with an idea. "We should prank her. The prank of all pranks!"

"Like that would end well. She'd probably send Elvis chasing after us in his sheriff costume."

Elvis was Mrs. Parish's German shepherd. Any student who'd ever been sent to the principal's office knew about him because professional glamour shots of the poor pooch covered the room. And Mrs. Parish was usually eager to talk to us about his latest look as a cowboy, ballerina, or mermaid. Something absolutely no one wanted to do until the McNutts, who frequently found themselves in the principal's puke-green chairs, discovered that asking about the dog was a surefire way to avoid returning to class.

"I'm pretty sure we can outrun Elvis," Johnny said. "Besides, we'll make sure we don't get caught."

"C'mon! Mrs. Parish always finds out! Remember the big show she made of updating your permanent record when you dropped mints into that two-liter soda?"

"I did *not* damage school property. The carpet was already that ugly before the holiday concert."

"But your new teachers will think you did when Mrs. Parish sends over the files."

"What is her problem?" Johnny asked. It was the age-old question that had puzzled FDR students since Mrs. Parish's first day as principal in 1974.

I sighed, plopped down on a swing, and kicked a lone fluffy white dandelion. "I wonder what her permanent record looks like."

"Let's steal it! We'll photocopy it and share it with everyone!"

"And how are we going to break into the mayor's office?"

"Is that where permanent records go?"

"They're permanent, so they go somewhere forever," I said. "The president is too busy to store 'em, so the mayor probably keeps 'em."

"Yeah." Johnny sat down on the swing next to me and blankly gazed across the lawn. "I bet I can jump farther than you."

I accepted his challenge right away and took to the air in my squeaky swing. As a matter of principle, no one was going to swing higher or jump farther than me in my own backyard!

Johnny quickly rocketed toward the sky. "My mom keeps trying to make me feel better about being the New Kid by telling me that Lenah Higbee is a fresh start and a clean slate."

"Ugh, but I don't want a fresh start for one lousy year before another fresh start in middle school," I said. "Mrs. Parish shipping our permanent records isn't a clean slate anyway."

"No kidding."

Kicking my legs out, I leaned way back and soared in sync with Johnny. "Ready? Get set . . . *jump!*"

As I flew through the air, the threatening clouds of permanent records suddenly parted to reveal a blue sky.

I heard music!

I smelled lilacs!

I received a thumbs-up from a squirrel!

I knew exactly what the Sherlock Pines Gang had to do to take charge of our future and throw a wrench into Mrs. Parish's unfair scheme.

"Johnny!" I said, landing next to him in the grass. "I know what—"

"Yes! My feet are in front of yours," he shouted. "I win!"

I waved aside his gloating. "Yeah, yeah, yeah, you jumped farther—listen to me. We might not be able to break into the mayor's office, but we can certainly break into the teachers' lounge."

Johnny stared at me like I was insane. "The *teachers' lounge*?"

I looked at him with a confident smile. "We're going to steal our permanent records."

CHAPTER FOUR

The Gang Hatches a Plan

▼ ▲ ▼ ▲ ▼

"Becky, you have lost your mind!" Diana said.

She was sitting with the Sherlock Pines Gang inside my backyard tree house, our official hideout where we plot adventures, solve cases, and avoid Meschinos. We had nicknamed it 221B like the headquarters of Sherlock and Watson, but we didn't have a sign like they did (ours being a top secret location and all). The only outside decoration was a golden pom-pom that I occasionally tied to the empty flagpole to signal an emergency meeting.

Unsurprisingly, Diana thought I'd gone bonkers when she found out why I had hung the pom-pom.

"There's no way!" she continued. "Mrs. Parish said if we steal anything before FDR closes, she'll add it to our permanent records."

"We're *stealing* our permanent records," I said. "Mrs. Parish can't add anything."

"Even if we're able to break in, we'll never make it past the protective lasers," Gina said.

"Yes, we can," Johnny said. "Becky's plan is really good."

"You can count on us," Bobby told me, gesturing to his brother.

Tommy nodded. "I've always wanted to sneak into the teachers' lounge to see what they're hiding in there."

"Lasers," Gina said as she messed around with a radio antenna.

"Gina, there are no lasers in the teachers' lounge," I said.

"You don't know for sure. What if Mrs. Parish installed the special kid-shrinking kind of lasers?"

"How many times do I have to tell you—*Honey, I Shrunk the Kids* is not real."

"I don't want to end up itty-bitty and get chased by a scorpion."

I sighed. "Fine, if the teachers' lounge is protected by lasers, I promise you will not have to go anywhere near the lasers."

"Then I'm in," Gina said, finally tuning in the Top 40 station.

"Stealing our permanent records won't keep FDR open, will it?" Diana asked.

"No, we would need a ton of money to keep school open," I said. "But—"

"They're our *permanent records*," Diana said. "Someone will find out we stole them, and we'll be in detention for the rest of our lives."

"There's nothing to worry about. We simply remove our files, and Mrs. Parish will never notice anything is missing before school closes," I said.

Candice turned to Diana. "It will look like they were lost in the move, like my idea for taking library books."

Diana still wasn't on board. "Mrs. Parish said—"

I took a deep breath. "If Mrs. Parish and the school district are going to rip us apart, without us voting on it by the way, and make us be the New Kids at new schools—"

"With 'clean slates,'" Johnny said, making air quotes with his hands.

"Then we are going to be the ones who wipe our slates clean," I said. "Completely clean."

"And we're allowed to steal our permanent records," Bobby said. "It says so in the constitution. Tell her, Tommy."

He cleared his throat for his dramatic performance. "When in the course of human events, it becomes necessary to dissolve the power that grown-ups have over kids, kids can steal their permanent records. Case closed. Thomas Jefferson said so."

"Look it up in the *World Book Encyclopedia*," Bobby told Diana.

"Exactly!" I said. "Read about it when you get home."

If Tommy could quote a law from the constitution, I figured it must be true. Over the years, he and his brother had established themselves as experts in explaining kids' constitutional rights, especially if they related to recess, report cards, and the dreaded mile run.

Diana thought it over. "I guess we are kind of like Matilda."

"What's a Matilda?" Tommy asked.

"She's a character in a book," Gina said.

"Is she in the Goosebumps books?" Bobby asked.

"We only read Goosebumps," Tommy said.

"Matilda has her own book," I said.

"And in that book, she stands up to the evil principal and wins," Diana said. A smile spread across her face. "OK, Becky. Let's do this!"

▲ ▼ ▲

We spent the evening in 221B discussing how to successfully sneak into the teachers' lounge and swipe our files. One false move and we would be toast, with the scariest permanent-record update of all time. It'd be so crazy awful that future generations would think the Legend of What Happened to the Kids Who Got Caught Stealing Their Permanent Records was just an outrageous tall tale that teachers used to scare students.

The only problem was that my mom kept yelling at me to come inside for dinner. She finally stopped bothering me when I said we were working on a group project that was half of our grade. Playing the homework card worked so well that Mom even ordered pizza to give us extra energy to complete the "very important assignment."

As the gang devoured three delivery pizzas and two two-liters, I went over the plan that Johnny and I had created for the mission to steal our permanent records, a.k.a. Operation Parish Stinks.

"This Friday is the day," I said.

"And that day is D-day," Johnny said.

"What is D-day?" Tommy asked.

Johnny explained the puzzling term. "It's what grown-ups say for an important event. You call something D-day when you're planning to do something big."

"Then it should be b-day for big day," Gina said.

"Gina!" Candice yelped as she wiped pizza sauce from her cheek. "Say it, don't spray it."

"We can't call it b-day because *b-day* means birthday and it's nobody's birthday," Diana said.

"That's why we're calling it D-day," Johnny said.

"No, Johnny—see, I told you. That name is too confusing," I said. "Everybody, we are not calling it D-day. We are calling it *Friday*. This Friday, May 28, 1993."

"You should have said Friday to begin with, Becky," Tommy said.

"I did!"

Sheesh, I finally understood how Mrs. Andrews felt when she tried to get us to focus on social studies, but all anyone wanted to do was talk about whether french toast sticks were on the lunch menu.

"Is there any pepperoni left?" Diana asked.

Candice bit into the crust she was holding. "Not anymore."

In a stunning breach of the Law of Kids, Diana leaned over to grab a slice of cheese.

Bobby yanked the box away the second her fingers crossed into cheese airspace. "You can't have cheese! I didn't eat any of your pepperoni."

"But there's no pepperoni left," Diana said.

"Tough luck. Cheese pizza is only for people who eat cheese."

"No it's not."

"Yes it is! Cheese is always for people who only eat cheese. You can't have any."

"Whatever," Diana said, retreating to her spot. But she was hungry and ticked off, so she went in for the kill. "When I get home, I can eat some of the triple-chocolate-fudge cake that I won in the PTO cakewalk."

Bobby did not appreciate the reminder. "You only won 'cause you pushed me out of the way when the music stopped."

Diana rubbed her tummy and licked her lips. "That cake is the most delicious cake I have ever had."

"Just you wait for next year. I'm gonna make sure you're the one who gets stuck with Mrs. Meschino's peanut brittle."

"Ooh, I'm scared."

"You should be! Peanut brittle is just a buncha nuts pretending to be dessert."

"Uh, *hello*," I said. "There is no cakewalk next year."

When faced with that bummer of reality, the two of them stopped arguing. But Diana interpreted the silence as a truce and tried again. "Can I have some cheese?"

"No!"

She angrily stuck her tongue out at Bobby.

"Hey!" Johnny said. "Becky is trying to explain the mission, and you guys will blow the whole operation if you don't listen."

I checked my watch and noticed that time had flown by. "We only have a few minutes before my mom starts hollering about bedtime."

"Sorry, Becky," Diana said. "Go on."

"OK, so Friday—this Friday—is the start of Memorial Day vacation. Teachers will have their guard down after the final bell because they wanna get out of there as much as we do."

"Making it the perfect time to break into the teachers' lounge," Johnny said.

"We need to prepare just like Sherlock and Watson would. Which means we have to observe who goes in there at the end of the day, and we have to confirm where the records are in the room," I said. "Bring notepads so you can write down names and times."

"Should I bring my notepad with the neon painting of dolphins or my notepad with the photograph of dolphins?" Gina asked. "The painting one is bigger but the photo one flips open like the kind reporters use, so it looks more official."

"Is one of them already at school?" I asked.

"Yes."

"Use that one."

"Okeydoke."

"Enough about notepads! What's the plan?" Tommy begged. "Does it involve squirt guns? Because mine's still broken from our last mission."

"No squirt guns needed this time," Johnny said.

I lowered my voice to a conspiratorial tone. "At three forty-five on Friday, after everyone leaves, I will sneak into the teachers' lounge. I'll be alone, so I'll bring a walkie-talkie with me."

"And I'll have the other one 'cause I'm the lookout," Johnny said.

"While I'm searching for the records, Gina, Diana, and Candice will stand at the entrance to the teachers' lounge and distract anyone who tries to enter when I'm inside."

"No problem. Teachers are easy to distract," Candice said.

"McNutts," I said. "You'll hang around Gina, Diana, and Candice and create an emergency diversion in case they need one."

"We should have a code word so they know if we need help," Diana said.

"Soda. Cups. Crusts!" Gina said, naming things that she was holding in her hands.

"Gina, it can't be something you might actually say," I said.

"Canoe! Coffee! Carrots!"

"How about Yamaguchi?" Diana asked.

"I like it," Candice said. "We're not going to accidentally talk about Kristi Yamaguchi."

"Well now I won't," Gina said.

"Who?" Bobby asked.

"Kristi Yamaguchi. She won a gold medal for figure skating last year," Candice said. "How do you not know Kristi Yamaguchi?"

"The only Olympics I watched was Dream Team basketball," Bobby said.

Tommy turned to his brother. "I think she's the girl on the cereal box Mom bought."

"It doesn't matter if you know her," Diana said. "You only have to remember to distract people if any of us say *Yamaguchi*."

"Gotcha," Bobby said. "If we hear you say that, we release a bunch of chipmunks to run around like crazy."

"No, don't do that again!" I said. "You can't do anything that Mrs. Parish will want to put on your permanent records because then she'll find out they're missing."

"What should we do?" Tommy asked.

"Don't *do* anything," I said. "Threaten to do something. Or pretend you're hurt."

"That's easy," Bobby said as he punched Tommy on the arm.

"Ow!" Tommy returned the blow.

"Ow!" Bobby socked his brother again.

"Stop it!" I said. "You're distracting . . . ah, good idea."

The twins high-fived for coming up with a promising diversionary tactic that we nicknamed Slugging McNutts.

"Don't hit each other too much, because you can't get into trouble," Johnny warned.

"Once I find the records, I'll grab 'em from the boxes and then we run back here," I said. "Easy as pie."

"Argh, don't say that!" Diana said, face-palming. "You'll jinx it."

The porch door creaked open, and my mom hollered, "Becky! It's eight o'clock."

I rolled my eyes and yelled, "Yeah, Mom! I know!"

"It's eight o'clock!"

"I know!"

"Well . . . it's eight o'clock, Rebecca," she said, as if I didn't know that it was eight o'clock.

From years of experience in such standoffs, I knew that I had approximately ninety-five seconds to get my butt inside and go to bed. If I didn't, my mom would punish me by waking me up for school fifteen minutes earlier than normal.

I extended my hand to my friends. "Who's in for Operation Parish Stinks?" Everyone enthusiastically piled their greasy-pizza hand on top of mine. "One, two, three!"

"Sherlock Pines Gang forever!" we shouted.

CHAPTER FIVE

Intel and School Bells

▼ ▲ ▼ ▲ ▼

Preparations for Operation Parish Stinks began immediately. The sleuthing skills my pals and I had gained from investigating neighborhood mysteries came in handy the next few days as we cased the teachers' lounge. The best surveillance spot was underneath a black-and-white photo of a cuckoo clock, the most fascinating thing at school.

The picture's mythic story traced back to a time when a real cuckoo clock hung in the hall across from the teachers' lounge, and the school was called Liberty Elementary. (The name changed to Franklin D. Roosevelt in 1934 to honor the new president for his role in ending an unpopular law known as Prohibition.) The then principal, Mr. Grundy, purchased the clock since it had a top-hat-wearing, flag-waving bald eagle that cuckooed every hour. He thought a timepiece with such a cute decoration was the perfect addition to a place named Liberty.

Unfortunately, someone else did not agree with the hourly racket.

According to the Legend of the Cuckoo Clock, a teacher was driven insane by the noise and swiped the irritating thing one night in 1930. She or he ran into the woods to bury it but came upon a band of wily bank robbers, who stole it and traded it for a getaway car in the next town.

Over the years, occasional rumors cropped up of some kid who knew some other kid who had seen something in the home of some random relative. (All of us knew to always keep our eyes peeled.) But poor Mr. Grundy never saw or heard that little bald eagle again. His treasured snapshot of the cuckoo clock, which he had framed and put up in the same place as the original, hung above me during the final stakeout on Thursday.

As I sat there before class, I pretended to draw in a notebook while I watched the McNutts gather intel on the target. Tommy and Bobby were deploying all their charm but so far had been unsuccessful in convincing any adult to let them tour the teachers' lounge. The bell was about to ring when they took a final shot at trying to sweet-talk Mr. Lockett, who seemed genuinely perplexed by the obvious allure of the only room at school that banned kids.

"It's the *teachers' lounge*," Bobby said. "Why wouldn't we want to go inside?"

"C'mon, Mr. Lockett. You're our favorite librarian," Tommy pleaded.

"If I'm your favorite librarian then why do you two have a combined twenty-three overdue library books? Am I getting those back before school closes?"

Bobby nodded. "Absolutely!"

"Do you even know what books I'm talking about?"

"Library books," Tommy answered. "Twenty-three of 'em."

"My entire shelf of Christopher Pike and R. L. Stine has been empty since March."

"Sounds suspicious. You should check the security cameras," Bobby said. "By the way . . . does FDR have security cameras?"

"I know where my missing books are," Mr. Lockett said.

"Speaking of books," Tommy said. "Might I say, Mr. Lockett, this tie you're wearing with the little bookshelves on it is very librarian of you."

"I can barely see the coffee stain," Bobby said.

Mr. Lockett chuckled. "Heaven help me, I think I might miss you two. OK, one quick look, but you can't go in." He opened the door, and the McNutts eagerly shoved their heads inside.

I was amazed. Bobby and Tommy did it!

"Well? What do you think of the famous teachers' lounge?" Mr. Lockett asked.

Tommy pointed into the room. "Can I have a donut?"

"No."

"Can I have a hot chocolate from the vending machine?"

"No."

"Can I have that roll of tinfoil on the counter?"

"No."

Before Tommy could request anything else, Bobby gave him a nudge and gestured to something. The twins grinned, barely containing their excitement.

"You're for sure my favorite librarian, Mr. Lockett!" Tommy said.

"Definitely! Thank you, Mr. Lockett!" Bobby said.

The McNutts scurried across the hall and crouched next to me.

Bobby whispered, "The boxes of permanent records are in the corner by the couch."

"Awesome!" I recorded the details in my notebook as we huddled together. "How many—"

"No more screwing around," Mr. Lockett said. "Get to class. All three of you. Go!"

The McNutts and I heaved our backpacks over our shoulders and scrambled up the hallway.

"No running!" Mr. Lockett called after us. "Tommy and Bobby, I expect those books by next Thursday!"

"Sure thing, Mr. Lockett!" Bobby said.

"You got it!" Tommy added. He turned to his brother and asked, "What books?"

"I dunno."

▲ ▼ ▲

The recess bell rang at 10:10 a.m., and I was so eager to get the morning gossip that I tripped over my laces while careening around a corner with the frenzied mob. I quickly tied my sneakers and bolted outside toward my pals on the hopscotch court.

Candice was jumping through the squares and bragging about the good life in Mrs. Andrews's class. "Then she gave me a whole package of Flimflams because I could name all the Greek gods."

"No fair!" Diana said. "Mr. Khan made us diagram sentences all morning."

Gina flung the hopscotch stone across the blacktop for her turn. "Like I am ever gonna need to diagram sentences when I'm a dolphin trainer."

"You'll never get a chance to be a dolphin trainer if you blow our cover," Diana lectured. She turned to me and explained. "Mr. Khan asked her for an example of an interrogative sentence to diagram. And she said, 'How many teachers use the teachers' lounge after school?'"

My jaw dropped. "Gina!"

"Don't worry, he just diagrammed the sentence and started singing a song about adverbs," she said, disappointed. "Thought I could trick him, but I didn't get any intel."

I smiled. "I did! The boxes of you-know-what are still in the teachers' lounge. The McNutts persuaded Mr. Lockett to let them see inside."

"Really? Maybe Bobby and Tommy can convince him that I returned that super overdue library book," Candice said. "Mr. Lockett keeps asking me about it."

"The book your puppies ate?" I asked.

"Yeah," she said wistfully. "They chewed Princess Diana's face right off the cover."

"Sorry about spilling nacho cheese on it," Gina said.

Candice shrugged. "I still got an A on my biography book report."

"What if Mrs. Parish ships the files tonight?" Diana asked as she nervously tossed the hopscotch stone from one hand to the other. For several days, she'd been focused on finding any excuse to call off Operation Parish Stinks. "We might break in tomorrow and get in trouble for nothing."

"Nah, permanent records are Mrs. Parish's favorite things. She'll keep them until the last minute," Candice said.

"Enough about Mrs. Parish!" I waved the new cootie catcher that I'd drawn while half listening to my teacher explain ancient Greece. "Who wants to hear their fortune?"

"Me! Me! Me!" Gina shouted.

She and I sat on the grass next to the hopscotch court, and we read messages that ranged from the amazing (a date with a *Duende Teen* heartthrob) to the icky (a kiss on the cheek from one of Tricia Meschino's vile older brothers). I swore to Gina that it was pure fortune-telling luck that I kept getting dates with hot movie stars, and that it had absolutely, totally, definitely nothing to do with the fact that I'd designed the cootie catcher.

After we predicted all possibilities for ourselves, Gina and I started picking dandelions to put in our hair. We had a very short window of time to gather the flowers before adults got to them (or before they disintegrated into puffy nothingness). For some bewildering reason, the presence of dandelions was one of the scariest things on the planet to grown-ups. My dad's dandelion-fighting skills were simultaneously the most admired (by adults) and the most hated (by kids) in all of Sherlock Pines.

I was helping Gina stick blossoms into her french braid when she spotted something in the grass.

"A caterpillar!" she said, picking up the black, white, and yellow creature. "I bet it's going to be a monarch."

"And I bet it's going to bite you," Diana said as she and Candice joined us to pick flowers.

Gina watched the thing crawl across her palm. "It wouldn't do that, it's too cute. Besides, caterpillars are herbivores, so they only eat plants."

44

"Becky?" a familiar voice asked.

I looked up and saw one of my sisters, seven-year-old Tiffany, and Diana's little sister, Amber.

"Are you guys done with the hopscotch court?" she asked. "Amber and I wanna play."

"We're not using it anymore." I tossed the stone to my sister, who instantly lobbed it back. "Hey, I don't want to play hot potato."

"Meschino alert!" Tiffany barely got the words out before she and Amber took off running for the swings as if a kid armed with a Roaring Rucksack with H_2O MegaBoost 2000, the biggest squirt gun in the universe, was chasing them.

I turned and saw Tricia Meschino approaching with her annoying flunky, Rachel. When they got closer, I noticed that Rachel had started wearing a velvet headband to match the one on Tricia's head.

Meschino alert indeed.

"Gross, I can't believe they're putting weeds in their hair," Tricia said to Rachel but really to us. Like most bullies, she knew the effectiveness of insulting a kid in the third person right in front of that kid. "Bugs are going to crawl into their ears and eat their brains."

"Bugs don't eat brains," Candice said.

"Yes they do!" Rachel hastily said. "Bugs are gonna eat all your brains." As a loyal bootlicker, Rachel blindly believed Tricia's fact-checking ability on all subjects from brain-eating bugs to chain-letter curses.

"There are no bugs on these," Diana said. "I checked."

Tricia scoffed. "They're probably no-see-ums. That's why they're called *no-see-ums*."

Diana rolled her eyes. "Whatever."

"Leave us alone, Tricia," I said.

"Aw," she taunted. "Dull Becky Dulles wants to be alone."

"Dull Becky Dulles, Dull Becky Dulles," Rachel chanted.

Out of the corner of my eye I saw Diana remove the dandelions that she'd tucked under the neon scrunchie around her half-up ponytail. None of us wanted to give Tricia a win, so I admired Diana's ability to act super laid-back about examining the flowers for creepy-crawlies (given her hatred of creepy-crawlies).

"What is *that*?" Tricia seized the cootie catcher that was sitting next to me, and she laughed. "Dull Becky Dulles thinks she's telling fortunes with a silly piece of folded paper!"

"Give it back!"

Tricia opened my fortune-teller and a devious grin spread across her face. "Look, Rachel! Becky wants to kiss Sean and Will!"

"Barf! I don't want to kiss your brothers," I said. "Haven't you ever heard of a bad fortune on a cootie catcher?"

Tricia's mean smile disappeared at the suggestion that her siblings weren't crush-worthy. "Are my brothers not good enough for Dull Becky Dulles?"

"I'd rather kiss an electric eel."

"Sean and Will can do way better than you and your dopey spin-art clothes," Tricia said, pointing to the starburst of glittery paint on my T-shirt. "You are a total *Duende Teen* fashion *don't*."

"At least I'm not a weirdo who wears the same perfume as the principal."

Glaring daggers, Tricia ripped up the fortune-teller. "Bet your cootie catcher didn't predict this!" she said and threw the pieces at me.

Rachel laughed until she noticed that Tricia had already started walking away and couldn't hear her fawning praise. She took off chasing her boss, and the two of them wandered near a field where some kids were playing kickball.

I said a quick little prayer to Mount Olympus and any of the gods I had just learned about from Mrs. Andrews. But neither Zeus nor Athena was paying attention because zero stray kickballs walloped Tricia in the face.

▲ ▼ ▲

After the sound of freedom rang at 3:39 p.m., Gina, Diana, Candice, and I cut through the playground on our walk home. That was where I saw the McNutts up to their old tricks in spite of Mrs. Parish's warning.

Bobby waved his magnifying glass in the air for me to join him. "Becky! Come look!"

"This ant is really sizzling!" Tommy yelled.

"Ew! You McNutts are demented," Candice said.

"Yeah, that's gross!" I shouted to the twins.

"So gross!" Gina said. One moment later she tripped over a crack in the blacktop and dropped the Hullabaloo toaster pastry that she was eating. She picked it up, eyeballed it, and took another bite. "Five-second rule."

Tommy shrugged. "Your loss, Becky."

And it *was* my loss, because my strong scolding hid my secret love of frying ants in my backyard with Bobby and Tommy. But there was no way I was joining them when I was surrounded by every kid from school. I had a reputation to maintain. After all, I was only a few days away from receiving the coveted title of Big Kid. And even though I'd be stuck in the boonies at Lenah Higbee, without FDR's perks and benefits, I did not want to start sixth grade hounded by gossip about cooking bugs to a crisp with the McNutts.

"I'm starving. Can I have a Hullabaloo, Gina?" Candice asked.

Thanks to her cool mom, Gina always had a never-ending supply of toaster pastries. Nodding, she turned around so Candice could open her backpack. "Bottom zipper."

Candice unzipped the magenta pocket on Gina's bag and took out a package. She squealed with joy when she read the label. "I can't believe you have Summer Camp! It's sold out everywhere!"

Summer Camp, the new flavor introduced in April, tasted like a combination of cotton candy and movie popcorn. It was the perfect cheap treat to sneak into the movies for kids like me on a fifty-cent allowance, and I had already stockpiled enough to see me through June at the multiplex.

As the four of us crossed Baker Street, something in the road by the subdivision entrance caught my eye. I jogged to the large welcome sign that featured the Sherlock Pines name, a large magnifying glass, and several pine trees. When I got up close, I checked out the brand-new decorations: a bunch of toilet paper streamers and a poster celebrating the class of 1993.

But the decorations were not what excited me.

"The ninety-three seniors tarred the street!" I yelled, pointing to the glistening 93 drawing on the road.

The girls rushed over to see the new neighborhood landmark.

"Cool, they put a smiley face inside the nine," Candice said.

"Pretty gutsy to put it right by FDR and—ew—it's still gooey!" Diana yelped, accidentally stepping on the new tar. "Ugh, I just got these sneakers."

Gina tugged on a piece of toilet paper hanging from a tree. "I bet Sean Meschino did this."

I agreed. TP-ing was Sean's favorite pastime, and he had trained his younger siblings to be accomplices as soon as they could throw a roll of two-ply over a branch. The four Meschino kids trotted out their impressive skills for a variety of neighborhood occasions including birthdays, block parties, and the Last Day of School.

"Stupid Meschinos," Diana grumbled while scraping her dirty shoe on the curb.

Candice squatted down for a better look at the tar and smiled. "You know what this ninety-three means? It means we've almost seen the last of Sean Meschino."

"Woo-hoo!" I joyfully broke into my best Carlton dance to celebrate the momentous occasion. "Happy graduation, everybody!"

"You gotta throw your arms more, Becky—like this," Candice said. She demonstrated a perfect performance of the funny moves from *The Fresh Prince of Bel-Air*, and I joined her to dance into my recently mowed (and dandelion-free) front yard.

Something caught Gina's eye, and she immediately darted to the flower garden. "A monarch!" she proclaimed as she kneeled by the patch of daisies.

"Oh ick!" Diana said, lifting her foot. Her sneaker was now covered in both sticky tar residue and fresh grass clippings. She plopped herself down on the lawn and began scratching the gunk with a stick. "Stupid Meschinos."

Gina came running back from the flower bed and proudly displayed the treasure in her hand. "It's a big one."

Candice looked at the orange butterfly. "It's dead."

"Duh, it was dead when I found it. I'm going to add it to my butterfly specimen collection. Now I have five monarchs!"

"Why can't you collect something normal, like key chains or bookmarks?" Candice asked.

"I'm not going to discover a new butterfly species by collecting key chains, now am I?" Gina said as she pulled a magnifying glass from her backpack. "And when I find a new species, I'm calling it the GinaLeena."

"Diana, look—the robin flew away! I'm gonna check on the eggs." I removed my sparkly paint-covered backpack and hoisted myself into the maple tree by the front door.

"Did the blue jays get any of them?" Diana asked, barely looking up from her battle with the tarry, grassy crud.

I took a peek at the nest, making sure I didn't touch it or disturb it. "Nope! Still three eggs."

Finished with her shoes, Diana tossed the stick into the bushes and stood up. "Good. I can't wait to see the babies."

I jumped out of the tree and picked up my backpack. My stomach filled with butterflies while I anxiously swung the bag between my knees. "OK . . . I guess I'll see you guys tomorrow."

"Yeah. *Tomorrow*," Diana said.

"What's happening tomorrow?" Gina asked while examining the monarch with her magnifying glass.

"Seriously?" Candice asked.

I looked around for potential parental spies and whispered, "Gina! We're breaking into you-know-where to steal our you-know-what."

"I thought we were doing that on D-day," she said.

"Tomorrow!" I said. "We're doing it tomorrow!"

"Gotcha."

Tomorrow.

It was the most important tomorrow of all our lives. And I was ready for action.

CHAPTER SIX

Operation Parish Stinks

▼ ▲ ▼ ▲ ▼

Friday, May 28, 1993, was the longest day in the history of my entire six years at FDR. Waiting for the clock to tick down to the final bell was as excruciating as waiting for a slice of birthday cake while some dodo agonized over the perfect wish.

The day began on the *79* with the most important first step of every Sherlock Pines Gang mission—synchronizing watches. Candice was wearing her mom's spare, since she'd accidentally wrecked her own by dunking it in a carton of milk on Thursday. (The lunchtime bet wasn't a total loss because we learned that Diana was right: *water-resistant* did not mean *waterproof*.) But there were no numbers on the face of Mrs. Cohen's wristwatch, and none of us could figure out how to set the time on something without numbers. We eventually gave up and headed to school after Candice promised to stay near someone with a watch that didn't require a degree in rocket science to operate.

While walking along Watson Way, we completed the next step

of the mission—memorizing a bunch of top secret code names to use during Operation Parish Stinks.

Becky = Uncle Jesse	*Candice = Winnie Cooper*
Gina = Lily the Dolphin	*Bobby = Michael Jordan*
Johnny = Dick Tracy	*Tommy = Robin Hood*
Diana = Sister Mary Clarence	*Teachers' lounge = Batcave*
Permanent records = Surfboards	

The moment of truth finally arrived when the bell rang at 3:39 p.m. Following the plan, Johnny sprang from his chair and ran to the school entrance. I killed two minutes of time by slowly rearranging the *Duende Teen* photos that were taped inside my desk.

At 3:41 p.m. I stood up and signaled for Candice, Bobby, and Tommy to follow me into the hall. Gina and Diana rushed over from Mr. Khan's classroom as soon as they saw us.

"Is it time to go to the teachers' lounge?" Diana asked.

"Ixnay on the eacherstay oungelay!" Candice said in pig latin.

"We have to wait for the OK from Dick Tracy," I said, switching on the walkie-talkie that was inside my backpack.

And then we waited.

The hallway was empty except for the six of us. Being a holiday weekend and all, the other students and teachers had sprinted to the exit at the first sound of the bell.

The walkie-talkie crackled to life with Johnny's voice at 3:45 p.m. "Calling Uncle Jesse! This is Dick Tracy. Come in, over!"

"Go ahead, this is Uncle Jesse," I responded.

"I'm outside FDR and have eyes on the Batcave through the window. The Batcave is all clear. I repeat, the Batcave is all clear."

"Roger. That's a green light for Operation Parish Stinks." Full of adrenaline, I turned to my friends. "To the Batcave!"

I sprinted down the corridor, leading everyone to our destination. The McNutts took their position under the cuckoo clock photo and began loudly discussing a stack of baseball cards. Gina, Candice, Diana, and I gathered at the entrance to the teachers' lounge.

Pressing the button on the walkie-talkie, I relayed our whereabouts, "Uncle Jesse, Sister Mary Clarence, Winnie Cooper, and Dolphin are—"

"No, it's *Lily* the Dolphin," Gina said.

Candice rolled her eyes. "See, Gina? I told you no one would remember your made-up name."

"Correction," I said into the walkie-talkie. "Uncle Jesse, Sister Mary Clarence, Winnie Cooper, and *Lily* the Dolphin are outside the Batcave. Michael Jordan and Robin Hood are standing by."

"Got it. I see you," Johnny said, waving to us through the glass of the school's main door. "Who's Winnie Cooper again?"

"Candice."

"Don't say my real name!" she hissed at me. "That's the whole point of code names."

"Copy, Winnie Cooper is Candice," Johnny said.

"Argh!" She wheeled around and mimed zipping her lips to Johnny.

"Preparing to access the Batcave." I clipped the walkie-talkie onto the waistband of my shorts. Then I put on my mom's gardening gloves so I wouldn't leave fingerprints while breaking and entering.

The lettering on the frosted glass in front of me screamed TEACHERS' LOUNGE in big, bold, scary letters, and I completely froze. The fear of teachers catching me with stolen permanent records was nerve-racking. Even more nerve-racking than the fear of my parents catching me with Madonna's *Erotica* album, the one with the big warning label, which I hid behind my jewelry box.

I took a deep breath. And another.

Diana elbowed me. "What are you waiting for? Get in there!"

That little bit of encouragement completely thawed my cold feet. If Diana "But We Might Get Caught" Rodriguez was confident about Operation Parish Stinks, then so was I.

It was time.

"OK . . . I'm going in."

I had barely touched the doorknob when two first-grade boys appeared in the hall. They were slowly walking toward the exit as they argued about which dinosaur was better: T. rex or velociraptor.

Whipping around, I hid my gloved hands behind my back and leaned against the door. I tried to look totally relaxed even though my heart was pounding like crazy. And just my luck—the boys stopped right in front of me to attack each other with their favorite dinosaur moves.

"Ryan Meschino," Diana muttered as soon as she ID'd the velociraptor fan.

Candice confronted the invaders. "Beat it, rug rats."

"You're not the boss of me," Ryan said.

"We can be here if we want to," T. rex fan added. "My sister is in sixth grade, and she'll make you—"

"Hey!" Bobby waved his stack of baseball cards in the air. "I bet you two can't stand on one side of the hall and throw this," he dramatically pulled a card out of the pile, "to Tommy on the other side."

"Of course we can throw it across the hall," Ryan said. "We're the best T-ball players in our class."

"You can keep the card if you can do it. Let's go find out." Bobby quickly escorted the first graders away from the teachers' lounge.

Diana watched the boys disappear around the corner. "All clear."

I hesitated. I could still hear the little kids talking, and I was worried they'd come running back as soon as they finished playing Bobby's game.

Ryan cheered. "Told you I could throw the best! Gimme the card."

"Great job! Here you go," Bobby said.

"Aw, this is one of those crummy baseball cards that the fire-fighters hand out for free," Ryan whined. "I already have seven of this player."

"Let's see who else I have in here," Bobby said.

Candice gave me a nudge. "Go!"

"You can do it, Becky," Gina said and gave me a thumbs-up.

I had no more excuses to make, so I grasped the doorknob, turned it, and barreled into the teachers' lounge. I closed the door and frantically scoped out the room for adults.

It was empty.

I relayed the good news over the walkie-talkie. "Uncle Jesse is in the Batcave."

"Roger. Sister Mary Clarence, Winnie Cooper, and Lily the Dolphin are standing in front of the door. Michael Jordan and Robin Hood are back in position."

"Copy that. Beginning the search for surfboards."

Taking a moment to calm my nerves, I marveled that I was

actually inside the off-limits, mysterious hideout. There was a refrigerator, a vending machine, a coffee pot, a bunch of orange chairs, and a big table with a bowl of fun-size Knee-Slappers.

The teachers' lounge was just as fancy as I had imagined.

I noticed a bulletin board mounted on the wall next to a floor-to-ceiling bookshelf. A stern handwritten note from Mrs. Parish hung in the middle, and it was addressed to whoever ate her yogurt from the fridge for the third time. The note warned that a write-up of the crime would go in the culprit's file if she or he did not immediately stop and confess.

Shivers ran down my spine as I thought about Mrs. Parish adding to my file when I was a grown-up. The yogurt note was absolute proof that permanent records lasted forever and could ruin everything, even a job. Fired up by this extra motivation, I realized that Operation Parish Stinks was the most important thing I'd ever do in my entire life.

It was time to get down to business.

I zeroed in on the orange sofa that was in front of a window overlooking the playground. And sitting in the corner next to the sofa, was a bunch of boxes labeled PERMANENT RECORDS. Bingo! They were exactly where Bobby said he had seen them.

I raised the walkie-talkie as I rushed to the boxes. "I see the permanent records!"

"Uncle Jesse, confirming you have eyes on the surfboards?" Johnny asked.

"Yes! The surfboards! I see the surfboards!" I did not understand how Johnny could expect me to remember code names at such a thrilling moment.

The moving boxes were arranged in piles according to the new schools, and the records inside were organized by our last names. I found the boxes that I needed and speedily sifted through the alphabetical paper files. I used my pen necklace to cross off the names written on my forearm (I didn't want to forget anyone in the heat of the moment) after I ripped out each of the folders and threw them on the floor. Tommy and Bobby's files were the heaviest, and I needed both hands to pull those two out of the *M* box.

After I double-checked the completed list on my arm, I began stuffing the files into my backpack.

That was when the crisis began.

"Hello, Mrs. Andrews!" Candice shouted.

My. Heart. Stopped.

"Mrs. Andrews! How nice to see you outside the door to the teachers' lounge!" Gina said at the top of her lungs.

"Girls, don't yell! I'm right in front of you," Mrs. Andrews said.

And she sure was. I could see her shadow through the door's frosted glass window.

"Calling Uncle Jesse! Calling Uncle Jesse! Mrs. Andrews is at the door!" Johnny loudly whispered over the walkie-talkie.

"Shh! I know!" I turned down the volume on the device and began cleaning up at the speed of light.

"What are you doing, Mrs. Andrews?" Diana asked.

"I want to grab my leftovers from the fridge before vacation."

"Vacations! Let's talk about vacations!" Candice said.

"Look, Mrs. Andrews! I went to the state capital for spring break," Gina said.

It was the first planned diversion. I hurriedly restacked boxes while my friends distracted the nosy grown-up with their photo albums, which they had put in their backpacks just for this occasion. When I finished, I slung my open backpack over one shoulder and grabbed the McNutts' huge folders that were still on the floor. I held onto them for dear life and wished for Mrs. Andrews to disappear.

"That's great, girls," she said. "But let's talk about vacations when we get back next week."

In a flash, the doorknob turned, and the door was ajar.

Nooo! No! No! No! No! No! I needed to hide!

"Yamaguchi!" Gina screamed, to activate Slugging McNutts. *"Yamaguchi!"*

"Ow! Stop hitting me, Tommy!"

"Ow! You stop, Bobby!"

"Kristi Yamaguchi! I love Kristi Yamaguchi," Diana said. "She won a gold medal last year."

"Boys!" Mrs. Andrews shouted.

"Did you watch the Olympics, Mrs. Andrews? What's your favorite event?" Candice asked. "I like swimming. Sometimes I like skiing, but mostly I like swimming. Do you like swimming?"

"Tommy and Bobby—cut it out!" Mrs Andrews said. "Now!"

While the McNutts pretended to argue over who started it, I raced around the teachers' lounge looking for a hiding spot. But the furniture was too small to crawl under. And I couldn't fit behind the couch. And I didn't see a closet.

Mrs. Andrews opened the door a little more. "It's a holiday weekend. Everybody go home and have fun."

I sprinted to the bookcase and squeezed up against the wood so that the side of the unit hid my body. That was when I heard a soft click sound, and the bookcase popped open.

A closet!

I slipped inside the cubbyhole, then pulled the door shut. I put my ear up to the wall to figure out if I'd managed to escape or if I was destined to spend the rest of my life cleaning erasers in detention.

"But Mrs. Andrews, I have a question about Greek—wait!" Diana shrieked.

The attempt to keep Mrs. Andrews in the hall had failed because I heard high heels clacking across the lounge's linoleum floor.

"Becky's not doing whatever you think she's doing!" Gina blurted out.

The high heels stopped. "What about Becky?"

"Uh, Becky . . . ," Diana stammered. "Becky's not here. Why would she be in here? I don't—we have to go see Dick Tracy. Bye, Mrs. Andrews!"

I heard the Sherlock Pines Gang scatter down the hallway. As I listened to my shallow breathing, I noticed a thin beam of light pouring into the closet. It was a tiny peephole! I peeked through it and saw Mrs. Andrews take her lunch out of the refrigerator. But something caught her eye on the way out and she looked at the bookcase.

I was dead meat!

Mrs. Andrews walked toward me, and paused in front of the bulletin board. She ripped off Mrs. Parish's note about the stolen yogurt, crumpled it up, and threw it into the trash. When she finally left, the door closed behind her with a thud.

Whew!

Seconds later, Johnny's voice emerged from the walkie-talkie. "Calling Uncle Jesse! This is Dick Tracy. What is your twenty?"

Diana was shouting in the background somewhere near him. "Is she OK? Where is she? Johnny, ask her if she's OK!"

I juggled the McNutts' folders in my arms and yanked the walkie-talkie off my waistband. "It's fine. I'm hiding in a closet. I have the surfboards."

"Mrs. Andrews is still in the hall. Looks like she's telling those first graders to stop playing *Jurassic Park* and to scram," Johnny said. "I'll let you know when it's safe."

I hooked the walkie-talkie back onto my shorts. My eyes hadn't adjusted to the darkness, but the closet seemed huge since I didn't feel any coats or hangers. Sensing a table near me, I put down the McNutts' records so I could fish a flashlight out of my backpack. I switched it on.

"Whoa!" No wonder I felt zero coats. The closet wasn't a closet after all. I was in a storage room.

The thing next to me turned out to be a desk. It was cluttered with a ton of dusty old junk that reminded me of knickknacks at my grandma's house. Especially the 1933 Delta Sue's Dime Store calendar, which was hanging above two giant stacks of math textbooks. Two more stacks of books (taller than me!) were piled up on the other side of the desk. And boxes labeled ELEMENTARY MATHEMATICS were jammed into every nook and cranny of the room, except for the space in front of a blackboard.

Storing horrible math books out of sight in a separate room was the only thing Mrs. Parish had ever done that made complete sense to me.

The walkie-talkie hissed and crackled. "Dick Tracy to Uncle Jesse, you are all good to exit the Batcave! We'll meet you at headquarters. Over and out."

I grabbed the McNutts' permanent records from the desk and put them inside my backpack along with my flashlight. The bag was so heavy that I nearly fell when I pulled the straps over my shoulders. After regaining my balance, I gingerly looked through the peephole to ensure that no one was in the teachers' lounge.

The coast was clear.

I turned a big handle on the inside of the bookcase, and the secret door popped open. Trusting that Johnny was right about the empty hallway, I bolted from the Batcave and sprinted out of FDR as fast as my legs could carry me.

But I didn't run the quick way to headquarters. I dashed through Scotland Yard and jogged along the woodsy bike path to lose any teachers who might have followed me. When I was certain that I was alone, I opened my backpack and found my permanent record. I briskly flipped through the papers until I located my Big Secret.

Without hesitation I removed the single incriminating page from my file and stuffed it into a small pocket on my backpack.

Confident that no one had seen me, I raced into my backyard and safely delivered the permanent records to the Sherlock Pines Gang in 221B.

CHAPTER SEVEN

All for One and One for All

▼ ▲ ▼ ▲ ▼

"What a buncha lies!" Gina said. "I never stole glue from the art room to eat it. I'm not a freak!" She angrily threw her permanent record to the floor of 221B, where we were sitting in a circle around the folders. "I only stole glue to make slime."

"I'm next," Candice said, grabbing her file from the stack.

Before carrying out Operation Parish Stinks, the Sherlock Pines Gang decided that the safest way to look at our records was to read them out loud before destroying the evidence. Guaranteeing that we all had dirt on each other was the best way to prevent anyone from coming down with a guilty conscience and blabbing about what we'd done. It was all for one and one for all, just like the heroes in *The Three Musketeers*.

Except for my Big Secret.

I felt slightly guilty about hiding it from my best friends, but I didn't want them to be mad at me. I glanced at my backpack in the corner of the treehouse, where the evidence was safely tucked away.

Candice paged through her folder. "Absolutely none of this stuff she wrote about me is true."

"That's called libel," Tommy said. "You can have my mom sue Mrs. Parish for writing fake things. Says so in the Bill of Rights."

"Wait, this one's real!" Candice laughed and held up a sheet of paper with the principal's handwriting. "Last year's Halloween party!"

The all-school bash in October 1992 was one of those moments that became FDR legend. Everyone still talked about how Candice, dressed as a Rockford Peaches baseball player, terrified the little kids with her graphic description of what she thought happened in *Edward Scissorhands*—a movie she had not seen. Her mom received a kazillion phone calls that night from angry parents whose kids refused to go to sleep in case a guy named Edward was hiding under their bed, waiting to cut them into tiny snowflake-shaped pieces with his scissor hands.

"My little sister slept with the lights on for a week, she was so afraid," I said.

"But it's not what happens in the movie," Johnny said before pouring a handful of Flimflams into his mouth. "Edward is nice."

"*Nice?* How can he be nice?" Candice said. "He has giant blades for hands like the killer in all those scary movies."

"It's true! Edward Scissorhands is nice," Johnny said between chews. "And you know what else is true? It's my turn!" He gleefully dumped his permanent record on the floor and spread the papers around for everyone to read.

Bobby pointed to a disciplinary write-up. "Peppermints in a soda bottle at the school concert! That was awesome."

"Until it exploded and flooded the table of marshmallow squares," Diana said.

"What does that report card say about kissing? Who did you kiss?" Candice demanded as she strained for a better look.

"That's nothing. What are you talking about?" Johnny scanned the mound to identify and destroy Candice's source.

"You can't hide anything. That's the deal." She ripped the paper out of the pile, and her eyes bulged with alarm. "Johnny kissed Tricia Meschino!"

At once, the McNutts launched into a hilarious performance where they pretended to gag, vomit, and die of shame.

"Ew, *Tricia Meschino*?" I said.

"No! You can't prove it," Johnny sputtered. His tongue was stained blue green from the colorful candy. "It's not true!"

"Yes it is!" Diana said in a singsong voice. "I was in your class, and you kissed her cheek on Valentine's Day."

Bobby suddenly rose from the dead and pointed his finger at Johnny. "Tricia cooties!"

"Cooties!" Tommy shouted, jumping up so he could die all over again.

"I don't have cooties!"

"That's exactly what someone with cooties would say," Gina said.

"Especially Meschino cooties," I said.

Johnny threw his hands up in frustration. "I didn't know any better! She gave me a valentine, so I thought I was supposed to kiss her. I was only six years old!"

"Do you like Tricia, Johnny?" Diana teased before making kissing sounds.

"I think it's time to see Diana's permanent record," he said defensively.

"No problem, I have nothing to hide. I've never kissed a Meschino." Diana opened her file and groaned. She pointed to handwriting on the inside of the folder. "It says a.k.a. Toad Girl."

Toad Girl referred to a famous event in kindergarten when Diana accepted a dare from the McNutts to put a live toad into their teacher's lunch. As soon as Mrs. Patel opened her Caesar salad, the toad, along with a crouton stuck to its stomach, leaped into her lap. Watching Mrs. Patel scream while Diana chased the amphibian around the classroom was one of the funniest things that any of us had ever seen at FDR.

"I hate Mrs. Parish," Diana said.

Tommy plucked a paper from her folder. "No fair! You should have shared if you were stealing candy from Miss Warren in third grade. Even if it was Vaudevilles."

I grimaced at the thought of eating the salty black-licorice abomination that Fullalove had been selling since it opened up shop in the 1920s. Watching a package of Vaudevilles fall into my trick-or-treat bag was one of the most monstrous sights I could see on Halloween.

"I didn't steal Vaudevilles," Diana said. "I hate Vaudevilles."

"Everyone hates Vaudevilles," Gina said. "The only people who like them are my grandpa, Miss Warren, and—"

"Tricia!" Diana growled. "I was framed by Tricia Meschino, and now all my new teachers are gonna know me as the Toad Girl Who Steals Vaudevilles."

"No, they won't," I said, smiling. "They'll never read anything about it."

Diana's face lit up with joy. "You're right! Oh my gosh, stealing our records is the best idea you've ever had, Becky!"

Gina nodded and looked at me. "Even better than your idea to save soda cups from Betty's Burger Beanery."

"Hear, hear!" Candice said. "Free pop refills for life!"

Johnny raised his root beer. "To Becky and real fresh starts!"

"To Operation Parish Stinks!" Bobby said. "May our new principals be way less stinky."

And with that final toast, we clinked our soda cups in celebration.

"Go on, Becky. It's your turn," Candice said.

I pulled my record out of the pile, and Diana leaned over my shoulder to see what was inside.

And what was inside—to my complete shock—was my Big Secret.

Stunned, Diana stared at me. "*You* wrecked the balloon launch?"

I stumbled over my words as I tried to confidently bluff my way through an explanation. "I don't know what crazy thing Mrs. Parish wrote about me, but it's not true."

"It's not Mrs. Parish," Diana said, holding up the handwritten letter from my folder. "You wrote it."

The blasted letter!

It was the apology that Mrs. Parish made me write after I got in trouble. I'd completely forgotten about it when I had rifled through my file in Scotland Yard. The only thing I removed was the write-up about my weeklong punishment of cleaning erasers.

In my confusion over the Big Secret reveal, some unfortunate words slipped out of my mouth. "I can't believe I forgot to take that out too."

Johnny stopped glugging soda and glared at me. "*Too?* You took something out of your permanent record?"

"Not cool, Becky," Tommy said. "It was all for one and one for all!"

"You ruined the balloon release and then you lied and tried to cover it up," Diana said. "How could you do that to us?"

The accusation hurt me, even though it was 100 percent true. I realized there was no longer any point in lying to the gang about what I'd done. "I'm sorry! Everybody was really upset when it was canceled, and I didn't want you to know it was because of me. So I messed with my file before I got here."

"I don't understand. What happened with balloons?" Candice asked.

Diana explained. "It was the year before you moved here. We were going to launch balloons with postcards attached to them at the start of third grade."

"Everyone in school wrote a message on a card," Gina added. "The balloon would fly somewhere, and whoever found the card was supposed to mail a letter back to us. Like a modern-day message in a bottle."

"Oh yeah! The candy thing!" Tommy said. "Whoever got a letter from farthest away won a year's supply of Fullalove candy."

"Fullalove around the world," Gina said, quoting the marketing slogan.

"But we never got to do it because *someone* stole the box of special balloons," Diana said. "I can't believe this is why I never got an Irish pen pal."

"I didn't know you spoke Irish," Bobby said.

"I don't. They speak *English* in Ireland, Bobby," Diana said. She turned to me with a scowl and asked, "Why did you do something so mean?"

"I did it to save animals!" I said. "Do you know how many dolphins would have died from eating five hundred balloons from five hundred kids? Five hundred dead dolphins!"

The color drained from Gina's face. "I would've killed dolphins?"

There were few animals more beloved by girls my age than dolphins. And Gina was the biggest dolphin fan in all of Sherlock Pines, if not the entire tri-county area.

"Yes, Gina. You would have killed dolphins. We all would have killed dolphins." Then I described what I'd learned from reading *Park Ranger Ashley*, my favorite kids' nature magazine. "When a balloon pops over the ocean, it floats in the water like a fish. Dolphins eat it 'cause they think it's food, and their stomachs get filled up with balloons. And then they die."

Gina was shell-shocked. "I was almost a dolphin murderer."

"Well, I don't want to be a dolphin murderer, either, Becky," Diana said. "So why didn't you tell us about what you were doing?"

"Because I didn't plan it ahead of time," I said with a shrug. "I read a story about pollution in *Park Ranger Ashley*. I saw the box of balloons at school. I took them and ran."

"Now I remember the balloon thing!" Johnny said. "There was supposed to be a huge cupcake party afterward."

"You owe us cupcakes," Gina told me.

"You do owe us cupcakes," Diana said. "And how do we know you're not lying about something else you did that's no longer in your file?"

"Look in my bag. The balloon write-up is the only thing in there."

Diana dug through my backpack and found the paper that I'd hidden. "She's telling the truth."

"I swear—that's the only thing in my record that I tampered with. I'm sorry."

Diana excitedly reached back into my bag. "You have that new book about science fair projects! Can I borrow this?"

Before I could answer, a ton of bells exploded in merry jingles beneath the tree house.

"Booby trap!" the McNutts yelled.

CHAPTER EIGHT

Treasure Map!

▼ ▲ ▼ ▲ ▼

I whipped a blanket over the stolen permanent records as alarm bells sounded beneath 221B. The noise was coming from the McNutts' booby trap, which was made with fishing line and holiday decorations. They had set it around the base of the tree in case a teacher, a Meschino, or any other buttinsky followed us to headquarters.

"Battle stations!" Tommy ordered. Armed with water balloons, he and his brother each scooted to a window to surveil my yard.

"Shh," I said, crawling to the ladder to peek at the intruder.

"Becky!" an annoyed voice yelled from below. "I nearly broke my neck on these sleigh bells!"

Relieved, I looked at my friends and whispered, "It's only my dad." Then I popped my head out of the tree house. "What's up?"

"Why is there fishing line everywhere?" my dad asked.

"Fishing line? I don't know." I said, trying to play dumb. "The McNutts?" Sometimes that name was all an adult needed to hear. Just saying it usually answered a lot of their questions.

"Sounds about right," Dad grumbled. "Here's the pizza."

I hoisted three boxes of delivery pizza into the tree house. "Thanks! Bye!"

"You tell those McNutts to clean this up before they leave!"

"Yes, Dad."

"And tell them to return my rake. I don't want any more of my garden tools used for lightning rod experiments."

"Yes, Dad."

The bells jingled loudly while he untangled himself from the booby trap. Then my dad finally went back inside the house.

As soon as the McNutts declared the backyard free of parents, we tore into the piping hot, cheesy goodness. Operation Parish Stinks had left us dying of hunger, and Tommy inhaled two slices within seconds. He burped so loudly that his family's two beagles, Pretzels and Gizmo, began howling up a storm next door.

"Sounds like we're ready for the McNutts' greatest hits," I said.

Johnny pounded a drumroll on the floor, and the twins dumped their large files into the center of our circle. I was giddy with anticipation, like the time I watched them whack a piñata filled with king-size candy bars.

Candice pointed at some photos in the pile. "Is that the broken clock in the gym?"

"Yeah, that was when Bobby and I switched identities so I could sneak home to get my slingshot," Tommy said. "I knew I could shoot a hard-boiled egg over all the lunch tables."

I giggled. "Tricia Meschino sure had egg on her face after making that bet."

"The yolk really bounced off the clock," Gina said as she looked at one of the pictures. "I forgot how much it stuck in Tricia's hair."

"Check out this huge write-up!" Bobby cackled, displaying a lengthy report from his permanent record. "The whole thing is about the second-grade standardized test."

"Oh man! Mrs. Parish was so mad when we swapped the box of number-two pencils with a box of number-four," Tommy said.

"I don't know why she flipped out. It was a controlled experiment to see what would happen," Bobby said.

"What happened was that everyone had to retake the test with the right kind of pencils," Johnny said. "That stunk."

"But we all learned a valuable lesson about the one thing teachers aren't lying about," Bobby said.

"That's for sure," Tommy said. "They're telling the truth about filling in test bubbles with number-two lead only."

Diana selected something in Tommy's file that caught her eye, and she kept flipping it over and rereading it. Then she reached over and found an identical document in Bobby's folder. "Are these real?"

Without looking at what Diana was holding, Bobby answered like a goofy carnival barker. "Why yes, Toad Girl Who Steals Vaudevilles! Step right up and see the world-famous McNutt permanent records! One hundred percent bona fide Mc—"

"Tommy and Bobby both scored in the ninetieth percentile on this year's standardized test," Diana announced. In disbelief, she held up the incredible results.

I stared at the McNutts. "You guys are smart?"

"No!" Tommy yelled.

Quickly dropping his sideshow act, Bobby declared, "We are *not* nerds!"

"So we filled in a bunch of the right bubbles with number-two pencils," Tommy said. "Big whoop."

Bobby scooped up his folder and a handful of documents. "Would a nerd have . . ." His voice trailed off while searching through his record to find proof of his non-nerd status. "Snuck into Mrs. Parish's office to declare a snow day over the PA? Or . . . or would a nerd have put a dribble glass on Mrs. Patel's desk? Or . . ."

As he hunted for impressive write-ups, an old, stained piece of paper fell out of his hands and fluttered to the floor. I picked up the crumbling page and unfolded it. "What is this map?"

Bobby glanced at what I was holding. "Not mine. Is it yours, Tommy?"

"Never seen it before," he replied.

"It's a map of school when it was Liberty Elementary," I said.

"Lemme see," Bobby said, grabbing it from my hands.

"Careful!"

"That looks ancient," Johnny said as he moved closer to Bobby. "Ick, it stinks like my dad's bad breath."

Bobby read the messy handwriting in the corner of the map. "*X* marks the spot for loot if ye are lucky, but death awaits ye if not."

"For real? It says *X* marks the spot?" Tommy scrambled over to his brother for a closer look. "You guys, this is a treasure map!"

"That is not a treasure map," Diana said.

"I would never lie about a treasure map. Scout's honor."

"You're not a Boy Scout."

"Doesn't mean I don't have honor, Diana," Tommy said before he released another loud burp. "Excuse me. See? Honor."

"Here it is!" Bobby tapped the map with his finger. "*X* marks the spot at the end of the trail."

The *X* seemed funny looking, so I leaned in to get a better view. "That's not an *X*. It's a four-leaf clover."

"Maybe that's an old-timey way of writing an *X*," Bobby said. "It's still an *X* that marks the spot. Tommy and I know treasure maps, and this is an *X*!"

"Cool it! I didn't say it wasn't an *X*. It *is* an *X*. But it's an *X* drawn like a four-leaf clover."

Bobby turned to his brother. "You ever read about leprechauns drawing maps?"

"Nope, never read anything about pot-of-gold maps. They'd be really hard to follow 'cause rainbows are never in the same spot twice," Tommy said. "Unless rainbows appear in the same spot twice in Ireland. I dunno. I've never been to Ireland."

"If I had an Irish pen pal, we would've been able to write and ask," Diana said while giving me the side-eye.

My mind raced a mile a minute to connect the dots of the mystery map. "Guys, this doesn't have anything to do with leprechauns."

"But there's a four-leaf clover," Gina said.

"Right. A *lucky* four-leaf clover!" Exploding with excitement, I looked at all my friends. "Lucky Killarney!"

"Lucky Killarney!" The words simultaneously erupted out of Tommy, Bobby, Johnny, Gina, and Diana as they dove for the map.

"It is!" Tommy said.

"The treasure map!" Johnny said.

"Lucky Killarney!" Gina squealed.

"What's a Lucky Killarney?" Candice asked.

I stared at Candice like she had just declared that her favorite kind of pizza was frozen school-cafeteria vegetable pizza.

"Lucky Killarney," Gina said slowly as if repeating the words answered Candice's question. "This is his treasure map."

"Wait . . . I don't think we've hunted for Lucky's treasure since Candice moved here," I said.

Back when the rest of us were little, we spent lots of summers hunting for the fortune that people said Lucky Killarney had buried during Prohibition. We never found anything, but our adventures did prepare us for the big Lucky's Loot treasure hunt at FDR in 1991. (The annual event was basically a sneaky way of teaching local history to nine-year-olds.) My friends and I correctly followed our teacher's clues, and we were the first kids to discover Lucky's "treasure" (chocolate coins) hidden in the computer lab. Lucky's Loot was the best thing about third grade, even though we all had to give presentations about Nicky "Lucky" Killarney and the Prohibition history of our town.

I explained to Candice that Prohibition was the period of time from 1920 to 1933 when it was illegal to make or sell alcohol in the whole United States. And even though grown-ups knew that they could get into big trouble, millions of them still wanted to drink liquor like gin and whiskey. Since there was a ton of money to be made, gangsters like Lucky Killarney began selling booze in a massive criminal scheme called bootlegging. These mobsters also ran secret bars called speakeasies, and they became really rich.

"Sounds like that episode of *Young Indiana Jones* from a couple weeks ago," Candice said. "The one that takes place in Chicago."

"Oh yeah! The bad guy with the scar who kills Indy's boss at the restaurant—that's Al Capone. He was a real-life bootlegger in the twenties," I said. "And all the hidden jazz bars where Indy meets his friends, those are speakeasies."

"But Lucky Killarney's speakeasy was ten times better than wherever Indiana Jones was hanging out," Diana told Candice. "Lucky's place was really, really, really, really, really popular."

I nodded. "My great-grandparents used to go there all the time. They had to whisper a secret password to get inside."

"Because it was hidden in the back of McCoy Dance Hall," Johnny added. "That's what the Scotland Yard picnic pavilion was before it was the picnic pavilion."

Candice was blown away. "That is so cool that there were real gangsters and flappers in the picnic pavilion!"

"Lucky was the most awesome gangster ever," Bobby said.

Gina agreed. "Tommy and I even sat in one of his getaway cars on a field trip to the Tri-County Historical Society."

"We didn't get a chance to see how it was hot-wired, though," he said. "The museum lady freaked because we crawled under the rope."

I went on to describe how Lucky ran the speakeasy with his brother-in-law, Declan Doyle, the owner of all the land in the neighborhood. The two of them managed to keep the speakeasy filled with alcohol even though Mrs. Grundy, Prohibition supporter and wife of Liberty Elementary's principal, taught numerous dance classes in the same building. But Mrs. Grundy had no idea that Declan had hired her only as a diversionary tactic. The scheme was supposedly cooked up by Declan's wife, a teacher at Liberty, whose really smart dance class idea turned out to be the perfect cover story for all the comings and goings at her family's popular club.

And business boomed there for years. Legend has it that Lucky frequently boasted to his customers that he needed a treasure chest, just like Blackbeard the pirate, to stash his riches. But such cocky bragging about his successful bootlegging monopoly did not make him popular with jealous rival gangsters.

"Then one day in November, Lucky vanished without a trace," I said. "Taking the mystery of his treasure with him."

"No one ever found him or his loot," Bobby said. "And he was Scrooge McDuck rich."

"Diamonds," Diana said.

"Rubies," I said.

"Gold," Tommy said.

"It's all out there, somewhere," Johnny said.

"When did he disappear?" Candice asked.

I pointed to the date on the map. "1932."

"Whoa!" Gina said. "He drew the map right before he went missing."

"Wait a minute, hold on," Diana said. "If this is really the map to Lucky Killarney's treasure, why was it in Bobby McNutt's permanent record?"

"She's right. That doesn't make any sense," Candice said.

"Is this another trick, Becky?" Diana asked. "Did you draw this and put it in Bobby's file as a joke before you climbed up here?"

"No!"

"But you lied about your permanent record."

"And I confessed and said I was sorry. I didn't—this map is real! Straight from Mrs. Parish's moving boxes."

"It can't be real," Candice said.

"Says who?" Tommy asked.

"Logic," Diana.

"This is an honest-to-goodness treasure map," he said.

"Gimme a break, Tommy," Candice said. "How many treasure maps have you seen?"

"How many treasure maps have *you* seen?"

"Maybe this was Mrs. Parish's plan all along," Bobby said. "She discovered the map, she didn't want to share the loot, and she closed FDR so she could treasure hunt all by herself."

Tommy frowned. "She disgusts me even more than mystery meat hot lunch."

"But Mrs. Parish would never lose something as important as a treasure map," Diana said. "No way would she have misplaced it when packing up permanent records."

"That's true," I said. "She had all the files organized and sorted alphabetically in the moving boxes."

"Did you see anything else inside the boxes that looked weird?" Gina asked.

"No. I took our folders out, put them on the floor, checked off the names on my arm, then put them in my . . ."

"Backpack," Gina said.

"I didn't put the McNutts' files in my backpack."

"Becky, we all saw you take them out of your backpack," Diana said.

"I put them in there eventually but not at first." Images flooded my brain as I mentally retraced my steps. "Remember the storage room behind the bookcase that I told you guys about? When I got inside, I put the McNutts' folders on a desk so I could get a flashlight out of my bag. But the desk was all messy and I was wearing gardening gloves . . . I must have accidentally picked up the map when I grabbed the folders and didn't notice!"

"Why would Mrs. Parish keep a treasure map in a storage room?" Diana asked.

"She wouldn't!" Johnny said. He looked at me and I could tell that he and I were thinking the same thing.

"Because it isn't a storage room," I said, barely able to keep up with the thoughts zipping through my mind. "The bookcase is a secret passage to a secret room. No one else knows it exists. Not Mrs. Parish, not the teachers, not anyone. Except us and Lucky Killarney."

Wide-eyed, Gina said, "It's where he hid his treasure!"

"I don't think it's in there. Look at the map." I traced the line to the X with my finger. "The start is Liberty Elementary, and it goes for miles. There's gotta be a second secret door somewhere."

"Right, the first room is a fake in case someone accidentally saw inside, like Becky did," Johnny said. "It's like all the secret passages in everything, they're always—"

"Hidden in plain sight!" Candice and Diana said simultaneously.

"And Lucky was an expert in hiding things," Bobby said. "He hid a whole speakeasy in the picnic pavilion."

"Guys, I am telling you, this is Lucky Killarney's treasure map," Tommy said. "I've seen dozens in books, and this is the real deal."

A huge smile formed on Diana's face. "We're gonna be rich!"

"We can use the treasure money to save FDR!" I said. "The school district won't close it, and we won't get split up."

"We won't have to be Papermakers," Johnny said to me.

"And we'll all graduate high school together!" I was over the moon just thinking about it.

Tommy picked up the map and looked at it in awe. "I've been dreaming of this moment for eleven long years."

But before the Sherlock Pines Gang could go treasure hunting, we needed to put our sleuthing skills to use and destroy the incriminating evidence of Operation Parish Stinks.

CHAPTER NINE

The Memorial Day Vomiting

▼ ▲ ▼ ▲ ▼

The annual Sherlock Pines bonfire was scheduled for dusk on Memorial Day. And it was into that very bonfire that we planned to toss our permanent records for complete and utter destruction.

Ever since the neighborhood's first block party, generations of kids had passed along the handy tip of using the fire to obliterate everything from report cards to diaries to embarrassing photos. I desperately wanted to chuck my five-year-old sister's *Aladdin* soundtrack into the flames in 1993. (Crystal was driving me insane by playing "Friend Like Me" three thousand times per day.) But it was way too risky to hurl that cassette through the air on the same night I had to wipe my permanent record off the face of the earth without parents noticing.

And those eagle-eyed grown-ups were everywhere at the cookout, which was in full swing Monday afternoon on Watson Way. The closed road was filled with picnic tables, grills, games, and, as always, one bazillion bowls of potato salad. Every mom in Sherlock Pines had a different recipe that she claimed was the best, and it was a pain in the butt to keep track of which ones did not taste too this or too that or too whatever.

Scanning over the massive spread, I hungrily searched for my favorite summer food: Mrs. Juneau's smoked ribs. The platter of mouthwatering barbecue was sadly nowhere to be found, so I assumed Mrs. Juneau was still cooking in her backyard smoker. Totally starving, I decided that I was willing to eat my mom's potato salad, even though it had too many chives. I scooped into the big blue bowl avoiding the oniony green bits just as Mom walked over with her friend Mrs. Meschino.

"That's a cute top you're wearing, Becky," Mrs. Meschino said. "Tricia had a spin-art one like that last year when they were in style."

Ugh. It was like mother like daughter when it came to mean pretend compliments. Tricia had learned from the best, and the best was currently dressed in a sleeveless leopard-print blouse and glugging from a fancy bottle of fizzy water.

"Thanks," I mumbled. It took all my strength to keep my eye-rolling under control.

"Remember to bring your own meat when you come over," Mrs. Meschino said.

I pointed to the nearby card table covered in waiting-to-be-cooked hamburgers, brats, and hot dogs. "There's plenty of meat right there."

"Not for today, Becky," Mom said. "Mrs. Meschino is talking about when you go to Sean's graduation party on Friday afternoon."

"That's right," she said. "Bring whatever you want to throw on the grill for lunch. And don't forget to bring a few extras to share."

I'd heard of parties where guests had to bring chips or cookies, but I'd never heard of a party where guests had to bring their own main meal. It seemed typical of the Meschinos to host an awful bring-your-own-meat party on the first day of summer vacation. And although there was a teeny-weeny part of me that wanted to celebrate that Sean Meschino would be far off in a few months and the problem of the state of Arizona, there was no way I'd be caught dead at a Meschino party. Thank goodness I had a prior commitment of hunting for bootlegger treasure.

Operation Gangster Booty was planned for the same day, which was FDR's annual cleaning day. We figured the teachers' lounge would be empty because instructors would stay in their classrooms to keep tabs on PTO parents who snooped more than they tidied. Plus, we had a great cover story: Gina's mom and Diana's mom were volunteers who had already roped their daughters into helping over a week ago. If any grown-up wondered why the rest of us were at school, two official PTO parents could explain that we came along to help clean.

"Sorry, Mrs. Meschino," I said, trying not to sound too thrilled. "I can't go to Sean's party. I'm helping clean FDR on Friday."

"Tricia is helping at school, too, but only for the morning. There's plenty of time for you to come in the afternoon."

"I have the afternoon shift!" I blurted out a little too impulsively, considering I didn't even know if there were shifts.

"Really? You never help on cleaning day," Mom said in that voice she used when I knew she didn't believe a word I was saying.

I needed to use my best acting skills to sell the fib about FDR. "Yep, go ask Mrs. Rodriguez and Mrs. Lee. They'll tell you all about it. My friends and I are all helping on Friday."

"That's nice that you're volunteering at school before it closes," Mom said.

I smiled at my perfect performance. Much like claiming to be busy with homework, volunteering to clean school was a can't-miss way to get Mom off my case.

"But you can have lunch at Sean's party before you go," she said.

"Can't. I have to be at FDR when lunch starts."

"When is lunch?"

I had no idea, but I sure wasn't getting suckered into pity attendance for a Meschino kid's party. "Lunch is when lunch starts."

"At noon?" Mom asked.

"At noon," I confirmed.

"Good, then you can spend an hour with Sean," Mom said. "The party starts at eleven."

No! I was furious at myself for walking into my mom's time trap. "But Mom, I—"

"Excellent!" Mrs. Meschino said. "Sean will be so happy to see you, Becky."

"And we'll be at the picnic pavilion at eleven on the dot so Becky can have a full hour at the party before she leaves," Mom said.

Mrs. Meschino and my mom were two clueless peas in a pod. I knew the only way Sean Meschino would be happy to see me at his party was if I gave him a garbage bag full of his favorite things: toilet paper and shaving cream.

I was also pretty sure that Sean didn't even know my first name. Whenever he saw me, he always yelled, "Hey, Airport!" because one time he flew in a plane and landed at a place named Dulles Airport.

Stupid Meschinos.

▲ ▼ ▲

"Yikes! Even as a punishment my mom would never make me go to a Meschino party," Diana said between slurps of lemonade.

I was sitting at a picnic table with Diana, Johnny, Tommy, Gina, and Candice. We were chowing down on burgers, corn on the cob, and ribs from Mrs. Juneau's smoker. It all tasted delicious in the warm Memorial Day sun.

"Your mom is nuts, Becky," Candice said.

"The Meschinos are nuts," I said. "It's a bring-your-own-meat party."

"What does that mean?" Tommy asked.

"That it's gonna be the most terrible party ever," Johnny said.

I picked up a napkin and wiped barbecue sauce off my face. "I'm hiding in a corner with a package of hot dogs until I can escape."

"Be at FDR by noon. My mom said that's when one of the parents is arriving with the restaurant pizza from Viv's," Gina said. "It's lunch for everyone helping at school, including the teachers."

"The plan is we eat as fast as we can, and when Becky gets there, we tell the teachers that we need to go to the bathroom," Diana said. "Then we make a break for the teachers' lounge."

"I bet even my big sister will think it's cool when I show her the loot we discover," Johnny said before biting into his juicy cheeseburger.

"Everyone will think it's cool when we save FDR," I said.

Bobby joined us at the table wearing a stuffed backpack and a weird look on his face. "Hey, guys."

"What's up with you?" Tommy asked.

"Oh nothing," Bobby said, even though his smirk insisted that something was going on. "There's nothing up with me. But there's something up with what's inside my bag."

"If it's full of cans of exploding snakes from Otter's Joke Shop, just forget it!" Gina said. "I am not falling for that a fourth time."

"It's better than anything at Otter's," Bobby said. He checked over his shoulder, then motioned for us to lean closer to him. "What is the one thing that adults never let us have?"

"Coffee!" Candice said.

"Nope."

"Ice cream!" Diana said.

"Diana, that's only your mom who won't let you have ice cream," Tommy said.

"Ice cream for *breakfast*!" Johnny said.

"Nope, nope, and nope!" Bobby said with a mischievous grin. "I'm talking about the one candy they won't let us buy at Delta Sue's."

That got my attention. There was only one type of candy at Delta Sue's Dime Store that was slapped with an OVER 21 ONLY sticker. We didn't know what made that candy so special, but the fact that we couldn't buy it made it a million times more desirable.

"Yeah, right, Bobby," I said. "You don't have any Debonairs."

Bobby took off his backpack and unzipped it enough to expose his forbidden treasure: four boxes of Fullalove's Debonair chocolate cordials.

"He does!" Gina said in astonishment. "He has Debonairs!"

Debonair chocolate cordials were the holy grail of candy. No kid in the Sherlock Pines Gang had ever been able to taste Debonairs because of the dumb age restriction. We had also never figured out why a candy with the word *cordial* in its name (a fancy word that means *friendly*) was so unfriendly to kids. Plus, banning us from buying a specific type of chocolate broke a major candy clause in the Law of Kids. I had made this exact argument to my local councilwoman in a letter that I wrote to her several years ago.

I never received a response.

Johnny peered down at the boxes. "How d'ya get your hands on so many Debonairs?"

"Did you steal them?" I asked.

"It's not stealing if you take them from your mom," Bobby said.

Tommy's jaw dropped. "They were in our house? I can't believe I missed 'em!"

"We can't eat them here," Diana said. "The grown-ups will see."

We quickly disappeared into Scotland Yard to stuff our faces. After gobbling up a bunch of Debonairs, I didn't understand why they were supposed to be so special. Each one turned out to be a sticky, leaky mess to eat unless I put the entire piece in my mouth at once. Hands down, any candy that I'd ever collected during trick or treat (with the exception of disgusting Vaudevilles) tasted much better than the bitter Debonairs.

No sooner had Bobby wolfed the last piece than we saw the bonfire roar to life, lit by Diana's parents, the copresidents of the Sherlock Pines neighborhood association.

I looked at my Minnie Mouse watch, surprised that I had lost track of the setting sun. "It's time!"

"We have to clean up and get over there," Diana said. She frantically crawled around collecting the colorful metallic candy wrappers scattered all over the grass. "Help me!"

"I have to get the surfboards from my bedroom. I'll meet you guys by the fire!" I scrambled to my feet and hightailed it out of Scotland Yard.

▲ ▼ ▲

"Does everyone have a newspaper?" I asked as I swatted at ashes that were raining down from the night sky.

The Sherlock Pines Gang and I huddled together near the bonfire pit, located in Scotland Yard where Baskervilles Lane met Watson Way. We were hiding our permanent records inside old newspapers that Johnny and I had swiped from the bin of kindling. It was a clever trick that I'd come up with last year when I destroyed photos of the time my mom made me wear weird German shorts called lederhosen. (Why my grandparents gave me goofy shorts with suspenders from their Bavarian vacation, I'd never know.)

"Be careful when throwing the papers so that nothing falls out," I said. "Especially Tommy and Bobby—you two look like you're holding Sunday editions 'cause your files are so big."

"Hey, we got this," Bobby said.

Tommy snorted. "Yeah, it's not like it is our first time destroying school documents."

Diana nervously dog-eared her issue of the *Tri-County Herald Star Telegram.* "I don't know, Becky. What if someone stops me and asks to see what I'm holding?"

"You're holding a *newspaper.* And there are, like, a hundred of them already in the bonfire."

Rubbing her tummy, Diana complained, "Thinking about doing this is making me feel sick."

"Stop worrying and just do it," Candice said. She confidently walked up to the pit and threw her concealed permanent record into the inferno.

"See? No problem," I said. "The newspaper works."

Candice hustled back to our group and egged on Diana. "Well, go on. What are you? Chicken?"

By throwing around pretty much the worst accusation that a kid could throw, Candice quickly upped the stakes for everyone to prove their nonchicken status.

"I'm no chicken!" Johnny said.

"Neither am I!" Tommy said.

The two of them promptly marched off and tossed their permanent records into the blaze.

"I'm not a chicken either," Diana said. She took one step toward the fire and threw up what looked like fifty pounds of chocolate cordials.

"Yuck!" Gina whimpered. "Yuck, yuck, yuck!"

"Shh!" I said. "The grown-ups didn't notice yet. We have to . . ."

Oh boy, I had to take a breath because seeing Diana's puke on the ground made me gag. Debonairs were losing their appeal as every second ticked by.

"I'm gonna spew," Gina said.

I pushed her in the direction of the pit. "The newspaper first!"

"OK, OK!" Gina took two steps and threw her folder granny-style into the bonfire. Then she held back her french braid, bent over, and barfed. "Told you."

I turned to Diana, who hadn't moved since puking her guts out. "Give me your file."

"I'm never eating another Debonair for the rest of my life," Diana moaned as she held out her newspaper.

I grabbed it and stumbled toward the fire, but my vision was blurry from the smoke and rolling waves of nausea. I couldn't tell how close I was to the pit, so I launched the folder in the direction of the searing heat and backed up.

"Becky, you're gonna step in it!" Candice yelled.

"What? Did I drop some papers?" I glanced down and saw that my right heel was in a pile of brown vomit. I instantly felt the saliva building up in my mouth. Within seconds, I upchucked what seemed like one thousand pounds of Debonairs onto the grass.

By this point I suspected that the adults might be getting wise to a group of puking fifth graders. Pretty soon they'd stop arguing about potato salad and start investigating the retching noises erupting from the growing Sea of Brown Barf.

We didn't have much time.

I surveyed the scene through my hazy vision to make sure everyone had thrown their permanent record into the bonfire. Between heaves, I asked, "Surfboards! Does anyone still have any surfboards?"

That was when I noticed a McNutt twin about ten feet away from me. I couldn't tell who it was through the smoke, then I remembered that I'd already seen Tommy nuke his file.

"Bobby!" I yelled.

He was doubled over, hands on his knees, and he was throwing up. Bobby's newspaper was on the ground and the contents of his hefty permanent record were strewn all over the place.

Mr. Juneau began walking in our direction. "What's all the racket over here?"

I had to get the file before Johnny's dad saw what was happening! Gagging, I lurched over to Bobby and prayed that he wouldn't puke on me.

"Holy cow, how many brownies did you kids eat?" Mr. Juneau asked as he entered the Sea of Brown Barf.

Scooping up Bobby's vomit-splattered papers, I staggered toward the fire and lobbed the folder into the flames with all the strength I could muster.

Then I turned around and hurled the rest of my stomach onto Mr. Juneau's sneakers.

CHAPTER TEN

The Last Day of School

▼ ▲ ▼ ▲ ▼

In the minutes following the Memorial Day Vomiting, a swarm of meddlesome moms descended upon the Sea of Brown Barf. They swore up and down that our ralphing must have been the result of spoiled mayo, and they began digging into the Case of Who Left Her Potato Salad Sitting in the Sun for Too Long. Nothing could stop their gung ho investigation, not even Mr. Juneau's brownie theory.

Worried that someone might crack under the third degree, I quickly told my friends to confess to sampling every potato salad. Miraculously, the trick worked. Once the moms realized they couldn't pin the blame on a specific recipe, the questioning ended. However, the unexpected turn of events left them all fired up with only one outlet for their extra energy: the Mom Network.

By the next day at school, I learned that gossip about the barf-o-rama had spread through the area faster than news of a snow day. Teachers knew, for goodness' sake! The Mom Network had circulated the scoop so far and wide that one kid heard about sketchy potato salad before she'd even gone to bed that night—and she lived all the way over in Transylvania Forest.

That neighborhood was so far away that the trip to get there required biking uphill through two other subdivisions (Tall Tales Hollow and Land of Oz). But it was worth the sweaty journey to Transylvania Forest once a year for the spooky extravaganza on October 31. I loved trick-or-treating with the gang on Dracula Drive, although it was always a bummer to encounter grown-ups who lived in the land of Halloween and still handed out raisins. (Writing to my local councilwoman about this massive crime against the Law of Kids was near the top of my summer to-do list.)

Equally as horrendous as finding dried-up grapes in my trick-or-treat bag was trying to make it through the never-ending last week of school.

The greatest day of the year finally rolled around on Thursday, June 3, and a mix of exhilaration and sadness filled the halls. I would have been as upset as the other kids if I didn't know that the Sherlock Pines Gang was going to save FDR within twenty-four hours. But I did not expect to be sitting next to such a depressed face while I ate my usual peanut butter and jelly sandwich for lunch.

"Cheer up, Diana," I said. "It's the Last Day of School!"

"And it might be our *last* Last Day of School at FDR. Forever."

"It's not going to be our last day together," I said, trying to convince myself as much as Diana.

She looked around for secret spies then lowered her voice. "Just because Operation Parish Stinks worked doesn't mean that Operation Gangster Booty will."

"Well, now, with that bad attitude, I don't know if you're allowed to have any of these cupcakes," I teased. Then I opened a surprise container of treats. "Ta-da!"

"Can I have one?" Gina asked as she put down her apple.

"They're for everybody. I made them to say that I'm really sorry about ruining the balloon you-know-what and the canceled party."

Gina quickly helped herself. "You're forgiven."

"I wasn't even there for that thing, but I agree with Gina," Candice said, grabbing a cupcake.

Diana looked me in the eye. "Are you also sorry for the lying and the switcheroo?"

"Yes, I shouldn't have taken anything out of my file."

With a mouthful of neon-pink frosting, Candice said, "These are so good! Maybe I should bring cupcakes to Lifeguard Tom Cruise when we go to P. Tonnes this summer."

Last year Candice spent hours upon hours unsuccessfully seeking the attention of the cute P. Tonnes lifeguard, who looked like Tom Cruise. She had been in love with him ever since they made eye contact after he blew his whistle at her for too much splashing.

"I bet cupcakes will work," Gina said. "I once got my brother to do my chores by giving him a coupon for free ice cream at Betty's Burger Beanery."

Candice tossed the last piece into her mouth. "And everybody likes cupcakes!"

"Lifeguard Tom Cruise might not even be working there this year," Diana said.

"Jeez, Diana, stop being such a worrywart for, like, one minute," Candice said. "Lifeguard Tom Cruise has to be there. It's a water park. He's a lifeguard."

Diana peered into my container. "I'm just saying."

I decided to give her a little nudge. "It's the new Flimflams cake mix from Fullalove."

"Really?" Smiling, Diana selected a neon-purple cupcake. "I've wanted to try this, but my mom won't buy it."

Unluckily for her (and sometimes the rest of us), Diana had been cursed with a mom whose idea of dessert was fruit and yogurt. Even for birthday parties.

I leaned into the aisle between lunch tables to get the attention of Johnny and the McNutts, who were sitting on the boys' side of the gym. "Psst!" I gestured to what I was holding, and the twins lunged for the treats before I could even explain that they were I'm-sorry cupcakes.

"I want the green one!" Bobby said.

"No, I want the green one!" Tommy said.

"They taste the same," I said.

"Then I want the green one."

"*I* want the green one!"

I pulled the container away. "You're acting like babies, and babies don't get the green one."

Before I could end the frosting battle by handing the bright-green cupcake to Johnny, Bobby seized it with the speed of a frog snatching a choice bug for dinner.

"No fair!" Tommy wailed. "Now I have to eat an orange one."

"I'll eat it if you don't want it," Gina offered.

"I'm going to eat it," Tommy said right before he shoved the entire thing into his mouth. "I just hate orange."

Johnny eyed the remaining cupcake.

"Sorry about ruining you-know-what," I said.

"Huh?"

"You know."

"No."

"Do you want the cupcake or not, Johnny?"

"That's a dumb question." He reached for the final dessert and took a huge bite of neon-orange buttercream.

▲ ▼ ▲

Since it was the Last Day of School, we spent the afternoon clearing out our desks. Mrs. Andrews was in such a good mood about summer vacation (and her upcoming wedding-free hiking trip to British Columbia) that she played the radio while we worked. As an extra-special treat, she turned the channel to one that played Janet Jackson's new song and not to one that played old-people music from before we were born.

To the sounds of R & B, Bobby and Tommy dumped everything from their desks into the trash at warp speed and then huddled together on the floor. I assumed they were carving their names onto more school property, but I soon realized they weren't engraving chairs, desks, or anything else. They were each scraping a tree branch to a point with scissors. Something that made zero sense until I remembered an after-school fight had been declared between Lancelot (played by Tommy) and Luke Skywalker (played by Bobby) to see whether a metal sword beat a laser one.

Luckily for the McNutts, their sword whittling wasn't enough to register on Tricia Meschino's tattletale radar since she was too busy trying to mooch supply freebies from Mrs. Andrews. It was a real bonanza on account of FDR closing, and Tricia was determined to get her hands on school chalk, overhead markers, and the item most prized by all kids: mounting putty.

None of us had ever seen that precious sticky blue stuff outside of a classroom, even though it was way more fun to use for hanging posters than tape or pushpins. I had once asked my parents to buy some for me, and they claimed they didn't know anything about the "horrible blue goo that stains walls." But this was finally my chance.

"Mrs. Andrews?" I asked. "Do you have any more blue stuff?"

"Sorry, Becky. I gave it all to Tricia."

"Oh. That's too bad."

My trembling voice surprised me. I wasn't supposed to be sad on the Last Day of School. I was going to save FDR, for crying out loud!

I had to get it together.

"Tell you what—if I find more putty in my desk, I'll give it to you tomorrow when you come to help clean."

"OK. Thank you, Mrs. Andrews."

"And I promise you won't have to eat any potato salad for lunch tomorrow either!" Mrs. Andrews said, laughing. "Boy, I heard all about what hap—"

The final bell of the year rang, and everyone, including Mrs. Andrews, was off like a shot.

Except for me. I hoped it wasn't the *final* final bell that I would ever hear at FDR.

"Becky, come on!" Candice yelled. She was standing in the doorway and waving to me, the only other person left in the room. "I bet a quarter on Lancelot to win, and I don't want to miss the fight."

"Coming!" I peeled off the last *Duende Teen* photo that was taped inside the lid of my desk and tucked it into my backpack. Then I took a long look around my fifth-grade classroom and thought about—

"*Becky!*"

"I'm coming! Don't have a cow!"

Sheesh, so much for reminiscing.

I rapidly zipped up my backpack and hurried out of classroom 501 for the very last time. Joining Candice, I happily raced down the hall toward sword fights, sixth grade, and summer vacation.

CHAPTER ELEVEN

Operation Gangster Booty

▼ ▲ ▼ ▲ ▼

Ah, summer vacation! The greatest ten weeks of the entire year. A time to ride bikes, a time to roast marshmallows, and a time to avoid all things related to spelling tests and *el tiempo en español*. (I liked Spanish class, but I sure needed a break from the constant *"¿Qué tiempo hace?"* from Señora Katz.)

Summer vacation in Sherlock Pines had infinitely improved last year when Candice's parents put in a swimming pool. An *in-ground* swimming pool! An in-ground pool was the most exciting thing to happen in the neighborhood since I could remember. But building it took forever.

To kill time during the excavation, I helped the McNutts keep an eye out for frozen cavemen like Brendan Fraser in *Encino Man*. Alas, we didn't unearth anyone stuck in a block of ice—just a bunch of trilobite fossils. Even so, the long wait was worth it. As soon as the new pool was filled with water, Candice's house became the official summer hangout for the Sherlock Pines Gang.

Unfortunately, the first day of summer vacation in 1993 found me not in Candice's pool, but trapped in the picnic pavilion for Sean Meschino's high school graduation party.

"Becky, you're not leaving before you say hi to Sean," Mom said.

She was busy organizing snacks on a large table at the back of the room. White, gold, and purple streamers, the colors for Susan B. Anthony High School, waved in the breeze as pop songs played on a nearby boom box.

I checked my watch for the thousandth time and let out a loud groan of extreme disapproval. "Sean is one hour late! It is eleven forty-five and—"

"It would be rude to leave before the guest of honor arrives."

"It's also rude to not show up for your own party 'cause you want to sleep in 'cause you were playing video games until three in the morning," I ranted. "The only Meschino kid here is Ryan, and that's 'cause he's seven and Mrs. Meschino probably carried him out of the house and dragged him here."

"Tricia is busy helping at FDR—"

"Where I'm supposed to be right now."

"And she is coming when she's done with lunch at school. I'm sure she would like to see you."

"Ha! Tricia Meschino would like to see me as much as I would like to be here."

"You be nice, Becky," Mom said. "You're a sixth grader now, and I expect sixth-grade behavior."

Ugh! My mom's absurd friendship with Mrs. Meschino totally blinded her to the nightmare of that entire family on Moriarty Drive.

Ignoring her, I shoved a tortilla chip into my mouth and angrily chewed. As I thought about my escape options, I stared at the giant painting of Sherlock Holmes that watched over the world's worst party. This was not how I wanted to kick off my first day (technically) as a sixth grader.

I ate another chip and glared at my mom, who was carefully arranging a plate of ants on a log. It was so pointless; the only people who liked ants on a log were moms. No kid was going to eat celery, even with a fake-out coating of peanut butter and raisins, when there were real snacks in the same building. For someone who claimed to have been a kid, Mom sure didn't understand any basic concepts in the Law of Kids.

"I'm going to find Mrs. Meschino and see if she needs help with the grill," she said. "Be nice to Sean when he gets here."

I flashed a fake smile while squeezing a package of bring-your-own-meat hot dogs, ready to launch them at that idiot's big head the moment he arrived. "Yes, Mom. I will be sure to share some of my hot dogs with Sean Meschino whenever he stumbles out of bed and graces us with his presence."

"That's more like it," Mom said and walked away.

Once she was out of earshot, I rushed over to my sister Tiffany, who was sitting at a table behind me. "I need a favor."

"Do you want these ants on a log?" Tiffany asked with a mouthful of nachos. "Mom put them on my plate, and now they're getting vegetable goo on the chips."

"I don't want 'em. But can you do me a favor? I'll give you a new bottle of nail polish."

Tiffany began plucking the celery off her plate. "Maybe. And it has to be glitter."

"If I buy glitter nail polish for you, you have to promise to tell Mom that I'm still here at the party even though I've gone to school."

"Why do you want to go to school so bad? It's summer vacation."

It was a valid question, but there was no way I could tell her the truth unless I wanted everyone to hear about it. Tiffany was not known for keeping secrets when it came to exciting news, which was why no one told her about surprise parties.

"Mrs. Rodriguez and Mrs. Lee asked if I could help clean school before FDR closes." I glanced at my watch. Minnie Mouse nearly had both of her hands on the twelve! "I have to go now. Are you in?"

"You're lying, Becky. No one wants to clean for fun."

"The PTO is serving restaurant pizza for lunch."

"I wanna come and get some!"

You can't! The words burst out of my mouth, and I quickly calmed down so she wouldn't get suspicious. "I'm sure there will be pizza here."

"Uh, it's bring-your-own-meat. Remember?" Tiffany waved her package of hot dogs in my face. "I wanna come with you and get restaurant pizza."

"You have to clean classrooms to get pizza. And you have to be signed up to clean. But it's too late to sign up," I said, rattling off every excuse that flew through my brain. "Besides, Mom has to take you and Crystal to swim class this afternoon."

"So what? I wanna—"

I knew I had to offer something else to Tiffany before she blew Operation Gangster Booty over a slice of restaurant pizza. "I'll also buy your candy the next time we go to the movies."

"Next *three* times. And Summer Camp Hullabaloos don't count."

"Fine."

"What are you giving to Crystal so she tells Mom you're here?" Tiffany asked.

I looked over at our five-year-old sister. Crystal was sprawled on the floor and completely occupied with a conversation between a stuffed monkey in one hand and a plastic dolphin in the other.

"I'm not worried about Mom asking Crystal anything," I said, turning back to Tiffany. "Is it a deal for nail polish and candy?"

"Deal."

As I stood, I picked up one of Tiffany's ants on a log and pretended to enjoy eating it. I purposefully made eye contact with my mom to establish my presence, which ensured that it would be a long time before she went looking for me. With a smile, I forced down the celery and faked like I was walking to the punch bowl. But instead of stopping for a drink, I cleverly slunk into the crowd and disappeared out the door.

▲ ▼ ▲

"Where have you been? It's seven minutes past twelve!" Diana said.

"I know, I know! I ran from Scotland Yard as fast as I could," I panted. My heavy backpack, filled with treasure-hunting gear, had not made it easy, and I was completely exhausted by the time I found the Sherlock Pines Gang pacing near the teachers' lounge.

"It's OK. Everyone is still eating in the gym," Candice said.

I gazed at the slices of restaurant pizza in both of Bobby's hands. It smelled so good, and all I'd eaten for lunch were two chips and one log of ants. "I gotta get some pizza first. I'm starving."

"There's no time! We have to go now," Diana said.

"I'll be quick. You guys go ahead and start looking for how to open the secret passage. There must be a lever or something on the left side of the bookcase."

I sprinted to the gym and beelined to the pizza boxes from Viv's Pizza Place. With one swift move, I grabbed a slice of pepperoni and whipped around to run back to the teachers' lounge.

But I was instantly mom-blocked.

"Hi, Becky! So nice to see you!" Mrs. Lee said.

She was standing between me and the exit, totally clueless about how she was screwing up Operation Gangster Booty.

"Hi, Mrs. Lee," I said, silently wishing for her to scram.

"Feeling better after the bonfire? Such a shame about you kids getting sick."

"Yeah. I gotta—"

"I wonder whose potato salad made you all so ill."

I began inching my way to the door. "I don't know."

"Between you and me, I have a feeling it was—"

"Do you know where Gina is? I promised I'd help her clean that thing she was cleaning."

"You just missed her. She went to the bathroom."

"OK! Thank you!" I fled the gym with my pepperoni and dashed to the teachers' lounge. Normally I would have been annoyed about getting stuck with lukewarm restaurant pizza, but the cooler temperature made it way easier to stuff into my mouth while on the run.

No sooner had I touched the doorknob to the teachers' lounge than I heard Tricia Meschino freaking out about it at the other end of the hallway.

"Becky Dulles is going into the teachers' lounge!" she shouted with

the hope of alerting every adult inside FDR. It was as if Tricia's idea of the perfect start to summer vacation included the opportunity to tattle on just one more kid at school.

I burst through the door, ready to herd my friends into the hidden room that I assumed they'd opened.

But the secret passage was still closed!

Gina was banging on the side of the bookcase like it was a vending machine holding a package of Flimflams hostage while Bobby was yelling, "Open sesame!"

"We have to hide!" I ordered. "Tricia Meschino saw me come in here, and now she's going bananas."

"The window! We can escape through the window," Johnny said. He darted across the empty floor, where the permanent record boxes had been, and jumped behind the orange sofa. He rapidly ran his fingers around the window frame. "Where's the doohickey? How is this dumb thing supposed to open?"

Tommy picked up one of the orange chairs that circled the big table. "Open it with this."

"No!" I grabbed Tommy's arm, pulling him away from the glass. "We can hide in the secret room."

I hurried to the left side of the bookcase and furiously examined it for a latch, a button, anything.

"You're on the wrong side," Candice said.

"No, I was standing on the left when it opened."

"Exactly. So why are you on the right?"

"No, it's the . . . I guess I meant the bookcase's left side. Whatever—c'mon and help me!"

"What am I looking for?" She kneeled down to examine the

bottom shelves. "There are no candles or lamps or sculptures to twist like people do in movies."

"I don't know, Candice. I don't know how I opened it. Just look for something!"

As she and I searched for the unlocking mechanism, Bobby continued with the secret-passage-opening technique he'd read about in "Ali Baba and the Forty Thieves." Waving his hands, he pleaded, "Come on—*open sesame!*"

Meanwhile, Tricia Meschino's yelling was getting louder and closer. "Mr. Khan, get over here!" she shrieked. "Becky Dulles is screwing around in the teachers' lounge. She's probably spray painting the walls. Or stealing blue stuff!"

"Hurry, Becky!" Diana said.

I heaved my body into the shelves but nothing budged. "I'm trying."

"Be careful that you don't activate the lasers," Gina said, hovering.

"There are no lasers!"

"Recreate what you were doing last week when it opened," Johnny suggested.

I squeezed up against the bookcase like I'd done during Operation Parish Stinks. "I was trying to hide from Mrs. Andrews. And my arms were up like this because I was holding the McNutts' folders."

As I crossed my arms over my chest, I noticed something on the side panel near my raised elbow. I bent down and saw a faint carving in the wood. "It's a lucky clover!" I pressed it with my finger and it moved like a button. Instantly, the bookcase was ajar.

"The sesame is open!" Bobby said.

"It's really real," Diana marveled.

I smiled. "Told you it was real!"

For one brief moment, we stared, awestruck, at the secret passage to a secret room. It was a milestone in the history of Sherlock Pines Gang treasure hunting.

Our wonder was short-lived.

Seconds later we heard Mr. Khan's voice outside the teachers' lounge. "Tricia, what's going on? I was in line for ice cream cake."

In a flash, I pulled the bookcase wide open and motioned for everyone to hurry in. "Go, go, go, go, go!" As soon as my friends were safely inside the hidden room, I joined them and closed the door.

"My pizza!" Bobby yelped. "I left it on the table when I was trying to open sesame!"

"You idiot! Now they'll know we're in here," Diana seethed.

Bobby's telltale slice was in plain view when I looked out the peephole. Unbelievable! The success of Operation Gangster Booty hung in the balance all because of one lousy piece of cheese pizza.

But I was not surrendering my only chance to save FDR and keep the Sherlock Pines Gang together. Undeterred by the looming threat of discovery, I whipped open the bookcase, leaped from the hiding space, and seized the pizza with mind-blowing agility. I darted back inside just as Tricia barged into the teachers' lounge, yelling, "Gotcha, Becky!"

CHAPTER TWELVE

The Second Secret Passage

▼ ▲ ▼ ▲ ▼

I closed the bookcase door behind me one millisecond before Tricia Meschino stormed into the teachers' lounge. The secret room was pitch-black, except for my glow-in-the-dark sneakers and the tiny beam of light from the peephole.

Bobby snatched the pizza from my hand. "Gimme."

"Shh!" I hissed. Then I looked through the peephole and watched a pesky Meschino tear through the teachers' lounge with maniacal glee.

"I bet Becky is hiding behind the couch!" Tricia said. She raced to the sofa with a deranged smile that faded when she came up empty-handed.

"Becky? Are you in here?" Mr. Khan asked.

"Aha!" Tricia yelled, ripping open the cupboard under the sink. The shocking reveal she was hoping for turned out to be two bottles of all-purpose cleaner and a roll of tinfoil.

Unimpressed, Mr. Khan glanced at his watch. "All right, Tricia, there is a lot more cleaning to do."

"No! Becky Dulles is messing around in here and doing something she's not supposed to be doing."

Mr. Khan opened the teachers' lounge door. "Let's go."

"But Mr. Khan—"

"The ice cream cake is melting. I don't have time for this."

"Fine. My shift is over anyway, and I have to get to my brother's graduation party," Tricia said snottily. "Mrs. Parish will be there. She's my neighbor and my mom's best friend. I'm sure she'll be very interested to hear how you let Becky off the hook."

And with that threat, Tricia Meschino stomped out of the teachers' lounge. Mr. Khan shook his head, turned off the lights, and closed the door.

I stepped back from the peephole. "They're gone."

Diana punched Bobby in the arm.

"Ow! What's wrong with you?"

"You almost got us caught."

"We didn't get caught, so cool it," Bobby said. He took a bite of pizza while eyeing Diana suspiciously. "And keep your grubby pepperoni hands off my cheese."

"I don't want your gross slice of gnawed pizza."

"Then step away. You're so close that you're breathing on me."

"With pleasure," Diana said, emphasizing every syllable so that she breathed into Bobby's face as much as possible before moving.

"It smells like my grandparents' basement in here," Gina said as she turned on her flashlight and saw the secret room for the first time. "Almost as many piles of books too."

The cobwebby space seemed a lot smaller when it was filled with seven sixth graders crammed among towering stacks of textbooks.

Johnny flipped a light switch back and forth. "Broken."

"Never fear, the McNutts are here!" Tommy said.

He and Bobby unzipped their Bart Simpson backpacks and removed a pair of old basketball toys that I recognized from one of their birthday parties. The gadgets were made of wide plastic straps that were worn around the head like a sweatband. Mounted on each strap was a little net with a backboard plus a foam basketball tied to the hoop with string. To play, two kids wore the contraptions with the backboard centered over their foreheads. The goal of the game was to jump around and be the first to swing the ball into the net.

The McNutts put the gizmos on their heads and triumphantly displayed their nifty modification—both headbands had one flashlight duct-taped above each ear.

"Introducing the world premiere of McNutt Lights!" the twins proudly proclaimed. They turned on the flashlights and four beams of light flooded the room.

"Awesome," Candice said.

"We made them last night," Bobby said. "They're even handier than that laundry catapult we invented during spring break."

"The hands-free flashlights leave our actual hands free to dig for treasure or punch bad guys," Tommy said, taking a swing at an imaginary bad guy.

"You think we might run into bad guys?" Diana asked.

"You never know where they're lurking when there's treasure involved. That's why they're bad guys," he replied.

Gina turned to me with her hands on her hips. "Where is the treasure? I'm ready to dig."

"It's behind another secret passage, but there aren't any clues about it on the map," I said. "We should look for a second hidden button."

"I'll check the bookshelves on the wall," Johnny said. "Bobby, help me with your thingamabob."

"McNutt Lights coming right over!"

"Me too," Tommy said, joining the boys to examine the novels. Within seconds he flung a thick book off the shelf, and it crashed onto Diana's toes in a cloud of prehistoric dust.

"Ouch!" she yelped. "What did you do that for?"

"I don't get it," Tommy said, confused. "Pulling a book off a shelf is supposed to open secret passages."

"But you can't rip it off like that," Johnny said. He demonstrated rocking a book on its spine. "This is how you open a hidden passage."

"I'm kind of worried that you didn't know about the book thing, Tommy," Candice said. "I thought you were supposed to be an expert."

"I am an expert! That book's title is *Horseshoe* so I thought for sure it was a clue."

"Why would Lucky Killarney have anything to do with—?" I answered my own question before I finished asking it. "Horseshoes!"

"*Lucky* horseshoes," Tommy said.

"What else is lucky besides clovers and horseshoes?" I asked.

"I have a lucky scrunchie," Gina said. "I always get As on tests when I wear it."

"And I have a lucky baseball hat," Johnny said.

I shook my head. "Not that stuff. I mean normal lucky things."

"Lucky dice!" Diana said.

"Our dad has a lucky rabbit's foot," Bobby said.

"OK, let's divide up and search for a rabbit foot, four-leaf clovers, horseshoes, or dice," I said.

The boys returned to the bookcase and began slowly rocking each book like Johnny had showed them. Diana paired up with Gina to scour the dingy walls for lucky symbols. And Candice and I turned our attention to the cluttered desk by the entrance.

After plopping herself down in the desk chair, Candice picked up a gray hardcover notebook. "It's an old-school grade book." She wiped away some dust and read out the message that was handwritten on the cover. "Property of Mrs. Declan Doyle, first- through third-grade math."

I leaned over for a look. "This is the Mrs. Doyle that I told you about! The one who was Lucky's sister and a teacher at Liberty."

"Yikes," Candice said as she flipped through the pages. "Glad I don't have the same bad grades as Mildred Flausen. Or the name Mildred Flausen."

"I bet Mrs. Doyle helped sneak her brother into school so he could build this room," I said. "And to thank her, he let her hide in here as a trade."

"Must have been nice to have her own private teachers' lounge," Candice said, tossing the book back onto the desk. "You think the tunnel is right behind one of these walls, huh?"

"It has to be. The path on the map is so swirly that it's gotta wind along the whole school."

Several of the flashlight beams that crisscrossed the room began to bounce around so much that the place looked like Kidz Nite at the roller rink. I glanced over my shoulder and saw Tommy and Bobby playing basketball with their McNutt Lights.

Exasperated, Johnny tried to get the twins back on track. "Stop messing around with those things. I can't find the secret button if you guys keep moving the lights all over the place."

Bobby was jumping in circles. "I only need one more basket."

"Besides," Johnny said, "it's not fair if only you two get to play."

"I win!" Tommy pointed to the foam ball that was inside the net on his forehead.

I turned away from the growing argument about the proper use of McNutt Lights to focus on the desk. "Candice, you check the drawers on the right side, and I'll take the left drawers."

"Copy that."

I kneeled down and opened the top and middle left-hand drawers. "Math books and more math books."

"Same here. Old math books in all three drawers," Candice said as she shut the last one. "Boy, math class must have been such a nightmare before the invention of calculators."

"No kidding. Poor Mildred Flausen never stood a chance." I tugged on the left-bottom drawer, but I couldn't get it open. "This one is jammed."

Candice reached for the handle. "Let me—achoo! Ugh, all this dust is making me sneeze."

That was when Gina screamed.

I whirled around. "Shh! Someone might hear you!"

Gina rushed to the desk and placed a glass bowl in front of me. "I didn't notice them on the shelf at first because they were all dusty— but look! It's gold! It's a bowl of gold coins!"

Everyone jostled for a glimpse as I removed a dull coin and

rubbed it with my finger. A shiny surface began to sparkle in the flashlight glow. "It *is* gold!"

A flurry of hands reached into the bowl.

"Let me have one!" Diana said.

"Me too!" Johnny said.

"A real doubloon!" Bobby said.

"You think Lucky stole pirate treasure?" Tommy asked.

"Pirates are the only ones with gold coins," Bobby said. "No one else has any because the pirates stole them all."

"Lucky was always bragging about needing a treasure chest like Blackbeard," Diana said. "Maybe he stole Blackbeard's gold!"

Bobby gazed at the precious item in his hand. "Ahoy, Blackbeard!"

The only doubloons I'd heard about were the ones that pirates stole from something called the Spanish armada. I licked my finger and rubbed the coin to remove the last layer of ancient grime. Using my trusty magnifying glass, I searched it for pirate clues and zeroed in on the tiny text beneath a bunch of stars: Fullalove Confectioners.

"Aw, they're not Spanish doubloons!" I said. "They're Fullalove chocolates!" I peeled back the gold foil wrapper and held up the terrible evidence.

"Maybe it's only your piece." Gina furiously checked out her coin and came face-to-face with a circle of chocolate. *"No!"*

"They're all chocolate," Johnny said. Irritated, he chucked his back into the bowl.

Gina was crestfallen. "I discovered a crummy candy dish."

"These are exactly like the Fullalove coins that teachers hide for Lucky's Loot," Diana said, scrutinizing her piece. "Yuck, except this chocolate is covered in white stuff."

Tommy sniffed his coin. "Do you think they're still OK to eat?"

"Nasty! This chocolate is older than our parents," I said.

Candice grinned. "I'll give you a quarter if you eat it, Tommy."

Over the past year, Candice had spent nearly three dollars betting on food that she proclaimed the McNutts would and would not eat. She had won only once (the twins' kryptonite was soft-boiled eggs), but the entertainment factor of watching Bobby and Tommy chow down on weird stuff was more important to her than the outcome. And I totally agreed.

"Challenge accepted." Tommy popped the coin into his mouth with a smile and chewed. "No big deal. You owe me a—ugh, this tastes like dog farts!"

Candice cracked up. "Disgusting!"

"Where's the garbage?" Tommy said as he searched the room.

"There isn't one," I said.

"I gotta spit this out!"

"Don't spit all over the floor," Diana said. "There's no empty corner, and I do not want to stand in your drool."

Tommy fell to his knees. He grasped the desk drawer that I couldn't budge, and I heard a loud click when he yanked it open. Then he hawked a mouthful of chocolate into it.

I was horror-struck. "Stop! You might ruin a clue that's in there!"

"Gross," Diana said.

"Don't worry. The drawer is empty. Well, it *was* empty," Tommy said, wiping his mouth with his sleeve. "You owe me a quarter, Candice."

"No, I don't. You spit it out."

"The bet was not contingent on swallowing."

"*Contingent*? You and that stupid word you use so much," Candice said. "It's not a magic get-out-of-jail word for betting, you know. I don't care what your mom says."

Undiscouraged, Tommy continued. "The bet was not contingent on swallowing because you did not say that I had to swallow the chocolate. That's your mistake, not mine."

"Ugh, fine!" Candice pulled a quarter out of her backpack and handed it to Tommy. "But I have no regrets. That was money well spent."

Gina, who hadn't been paying attention to the dispute about betting terms, briskly walked to the blackboard mounted opposite the bookcase door. "It's the chalkboard. Becky—look!"

"I took a bunch of chalk from school yesterday. I don't need any more," I said.

"First of all, you can never have enough chalk." Gina plucked three pieces off the ledge and put them in her pocket. "Secondly, this whole wall moved when Tommy opened the drawer."

"That must have been the click that I heard!" I vaulted across the room and discovered a floor-to-ceiling gap next to the blackboard. "It's the other hidden passage! Gina, you found it!"

"And I'm not even wearing my lucky scrunchie," she said, beaming proudly.

I wedged my hands into the opening, and the rusty hinges screamed as I pulled the chalkboard door.

Diana grimaced and covered her ears. "Ow! That noise is worse than if you were scratching your fingernails on it."

"McNutt Lights! I need McNutt Lights!" I couldn't contain my enthusiasm about discovering not one but *two* secret passages within a few days of each other. It must have been a kid record. Heck, it was probably an adult record!

Tommy and Bobby rushed over to illuminate the darkness that lay beyond the door. The entire Sherlock Pines Gang crowded around the entrance and stared down into the abyss of the unknown.

"It's stairs," I said.

"To where?" Candice asked.

"Treasure!" Johnny said.

"Gangsters!" Tommy said.

"Australia!" Gina said.

CHAPTER THIRTEEN

Hullabaloos to the Rescue

▼ ▲ ▼ ▲ ▼

No other thrill I'd experienced in my life compared with the exhilaration of descending the creaky, dark staircase to embark on a real treasure hunt. With each footstep, I pictured the boatload of riches, hidden long ago by a bootlegging gangster, that my best friends and I were about to find.

After we gathered at the bottom of the stairs, I unfolded the treasure map and studied it to determine our position in the dank underground passage. At the same time, Bobby removed a collapsible spyglass from his backpack and expanded it to its full size of eighteen inches.

"Is that night vision?" Johnny asked, impressed.

"I wish! It's just a regular one that I brought to help find booby traps," Bobby said. He held the telescope far in front of his body and began tapping the ground as he crawled across the tunnel. "Get back, everyone. I need to clear the area before we go ahead."

Candice stepped out of his way. When she saw the map in my

hands, she asked, "What's the first clue? If it says anything about pieces of eight, that's code for pirate treasure."

I aimed my flashlight at the weathered paper and read out the initial hint. "Follow the hidden trail but beware the cursed goblin without yer lucky charm."

"Talk about a classic treasure map riddle," Tommy said, grinning. He raised his forearm and stared at his skin. "I'm so excited. Look at all these goose bumps!"

"Hold the phone, Becky," Gina said. "You never said we had to deal with goblins."

"Don't worry about it," I said.

"Don't worry—you just said there was a goblin curse!"

"I was right about no lasers in the teachers' lounge, wasn't I? Trust me, it's only a scare tactic. There are no goblins down here."

I wasn't the least bit worried about fighting my way past a goblin. Goblins were not real. And even if goblins were real, they were only around at midnight on Halloween so it didn't matter. The one scary thing that had crossed my mind was the possibility of a buried-treasure curse, but I kept reminding myself that we weren't excavating an ancient Egyptian tomb or anything. We were just on a quest for gangster loot buried underneath our elementary school.

"All clear. No booby traps," Bobby announced.

When I returned the map to my backpack, I noticed that Diana had wrapped a neon-green kerchief around her head and was tying it in a knot under her chin. Her ponytail stuck out under the fabric as a goofy lopsided bulge.

"What's with the scarf?" I asked.

"Yeah, Diana, you look like you're gonna go milk a cow," Tommy teased.

"Are you the lost eighth maid a-milking?" Johnny asked. "Are you looking for—"

"Five gold rings!" Bobby sang loudly.

"Ha ha! That was so funny I forgot to laugh," Diana said. She adjusted the bandanna to ensure that it covered most of her long hair. "We're in a tunnel, you dweebs. I don't want bats in my hair like in *The Goonies.*"

"Pshaw! The movie people just made that up to be scary," Candice said. "Bats don't nest in people's hair."

"No, Diana is right. I've read all about bats in *Park Ranger Ashley,*" I said. "That's why I brought—oh no! I forgot the garlic!"

The thought that a bat might build a nest in my hair was definitely gross; however, my main concern was the terrifying possibility of vampire bats. I'd seen them sucking blood at the zoo with my own two eyes, so I knew the stories were true. And I knew of only one defense against such bone-chilling creatures—garlic. Garlic that was currently sitting on the kitchen counter all because Mom distracted me and made me sprinkle paprika on two dozen deviled eggs for Sean's rotten party.

Stupid Meschinos!

"I have citronella," Gina said. She whipped off her backpack and got down on her knees to unzip it. "It works on mosquitos, so it might work on bats."

I shook my head. "It has to be garlic."

"Look up there!" Tommy said.

I instantly covered my hair with my hands but soon realized there were no bats in sight.

Tommy was pointing to a cable strung across the ceiling.

"The wire goes all the way down the tunnel from the top of the stairs," he said. "I bet we're supposed to follow it if we come across a fork in the road, and we have to choose whether to go left or right."

"I think you're right about using it as a guide. The map did say to follow the hidden trail," Johnny said.

Gazing up, Tommy walked forward and tracked the cable with his McNutt Lights. "I wonder how fa—*aaah!*"

The twin beams of light rapidly plummeted from the ceiling to the ground.

"Booby trap!" Bobby screamed. "Everybody freeze!"

I held on to my backpack's shoulder straps for dear life. "You said there weren't any booby traps!"

"He walked out of the area that I cleared!"

"What if the goblin got him?" Gina asked. She was staring down at her backpack, frozen in place while zipping it up.

With a pang of jealously, I realized that her hair was now protected by a P. Tonnes baseball hat. A baseball hat that we all got for free last year during the water park's grand opening. And one that was being totally useless right now on my bedroom floor when, for the love of Lifeguard Tom Cruise, I should have brought it along.

"Tommy!" Candice shouted into the tunnel. "Are you OK?"

An irritated moan emerged from the darkness ahead of us. "I'm fine. I tripped over a dumb hole."

"False alarm! Not a booby trap!" Bobby said.

Relieved to learn that huge rolling boulders weren't about to crush us to smithereens, I unfroze and walked over to check on the fallen McNutt.

Tommy sat up but didn't dust himself off because he was mostly concerned with the status of his prized invention. "Aw, man. My McNutt Lights broke!"

"Better the McNutt Lights than your head," Diana said.

"Duct tape incoming!" Bobby said. He tossed a roll to his brother, who caught it and began mending the cracked headband.

I spotted something gray and fluffy stuck to Tommy's face. "What's on your forehead?"

He plucked the thing off his skin and examined it with a flashlight. "Looks like fur and mud."

"Fur?" I asked. "From what?"

"The nest I fell into." Tommy aimed the flashlight at a messy pile of twigs, leaves, and fur about three feet away.

As a kid with a monthly subscription to *Park Ranger Ashley*, I knew that every nest had an owner. And I worried about what kind of owner had built the nest Tommy had crashed into headfirst. I hoped it was a really cute cat with lots of kittens, but I'd never heard of any tale where a kitten guarded buried treasure.

"Um . . . is there anybody in the nest?" I asked.

"It's empty," Tommy said, continuing with his repairs.

"Good! That's good," I said. "What about your shirt? Is that mud or . . ."

"Ew," Candice said. "Ew, ew, ew, ew, ew!"

"It's mud," Tommy said as he put the McNutt Lights back on his head. "All fixed!"

"I don't know if that's mud," Johnny said. "It looks like—"

"It's *mud*!" Tommy said. "Stop freaking out, it's not—"

"Behind you, Becky!" Diana shouted.

I swirled around, and the first thing I saw were the teeth.

The creature had giant teeth that gleamed like kitchen knives in the glare of the McNutt Lights. It also had beady eyes and a whip-like tail that was as long as the creature itself. And the creature itself was as big as my littlest sister when she was stuffed into a snowsuit.

"It's the goblin!" Gina shrieked.

"Stairs!" I yelled.

By the time I made a U-turn, Diana and Candice had already scrambled up the steps to escape the hissing beast. I hurried after them and was the last kid to squish onto the small staircase.

"It is huge!" Johnny said, clearly dazzled.

"Never in my whole life have I seen a rat this ginormous," Tommy said.

"I bet it would set a world record!" Bobby said. "I wish I had my camera."

I tracked the thing with my flashlight so that it couldn't mount a sneak attack against us. "Get a load of how it waddles around with that creepy tail."

"You know . . . now that I'm looking at it . . . I think it's an opossum," Gina said. "Not to be confused with the much cuter *possum* of Australia. Totally different animals."

"Whatever it is, I want to get away from it," Diana said. She yanked the doorknob at the top of the stairs. To her alarm, it didn't budge. "It won't—I can't open the door!"

Candice pushed her aside. "Out of the way! I'll do it."

"C'mon, then! Open it!" Diana said.

"I'm trying!"

"Try harder!"

"It's rusted," Candice said, pounding on the metal handle. "That's why it won't move."

Diana banged on the door, "We can't be trapped down here!"

"Well, we are trapped down here unless you have something to grease the handle with," Candice said.

"I have two cans of Zany Ribbons, if you want to try using that," Tommy said. "They were two for one at Delta Sue's."

"Party string? Your solution is *party string*?" Diana wailed. "This is it. This is the end!"

"Actually, Diana, this is the beginning. The end is down that-away," Bobby joked, pointing to the dark void.

Peeved, Diana gave him a dirty look. "My mom is going to kill me if I'm not home by four o'clock."

"We're not trapped as long as we keep following the map forward," I said.

"But how do we get past . . . *it*?" Johnny gestured to the thing that was sniffing at our footprints.

I had no idea how we'd move past the giant animal standing between us and buried treasure. But it turned out that I didn't need to worry. During the chaos, Gina had calmly unwrapped a Surprise Party–flavored Hullabaloo. And in unwrapping that Surprise Party–flavored Hullabaloo, a true hero revealed herself and saved the day.

"Hey, opossum!" Gina yelled. "Want a snack?"

She hurled the toaster pastry into the air, and it sailed past the beast. Sensing that a scrumptious treat had flown over its head, the creature devoted its full attention to chasing the Hullabaloo and devouring it as quickly as possible.

"Let's go!" Gina ran down the stairs and motioned for us to follow her.

And that was how we used a lucky charm to get past a goblin.

CHAPTER FOURTEEN

Creeps and Jitters and Scares

▼ ▲ ▼ ▲ ▼

Shortly after escaping the creature, Diana found herself smack-dab in the nightmares of every kid who had stumbled across *Arachnophobia* while channel surfing.

She'd marched straight into a monster spiderweb.

It took two minutes of shrieking and teamwork for us to remove one spider and loads of cobweb threads from Diana's clothes. It took another two minutes for Diana to douse herself in Gina's citronella spray, even though I didn't think that citronella scared spiders. And then five more minutes to assure Diana that there was nothing nesting in her ears.

I would have gone to pieces, too, if I thought there were creepy-crawlies on my head, but I wasn't surprised it took super long for Diana to calm down. She was always the one who overthought everything with mom-level anxiety during Sherlock Pines Gang escapades.

Like the time Diana left in the middle of dusting for fingerprints and took our only box of cornstarch with her. She refused to leave it with us because Mrs. Rodriguez was on her way home from work, and Diana was worried her mom would notice its absence. (Unlikely, since no one—not even Diana—could think of any reason for using cornstarch besides dusting for fingerprints or making Thanksgiving gravy.) As a result, the Case of the Smashed Jack-o'-lanterns went unsolved because a critter ate all the evidence that night while we were sleeping.

Or the time Diana wore head-to-toe camouflage for the mission to reclaim her stolen soccer ball from the Meschinos' yard. Her full disguise would have been great during the fall, but she stuck out like a sore thumb in July when the rest of us were wearing regular old summer clothes. No sooner had we stepped into enemy territory than the Meschinos turned on the sprinklers and began launching water balloons at the kid suspiciously dressed like GI Joe. Braving the steady bombardment, we nearly got our hands on the ball, but it was ferociously guarded by a cocker spaniel, who forced us into retreat.

However, Diana's overthinking sometimes led to the best ideas. She single-handedly solved the Case of the Car Donuts after taking an instant photo of the skid marks in the school parking lot, then matching the picture with the tire on the car parked outside the neighborhood Scary House. We congratulated her for identifying the culprit and then fled the scene on Adler Avenue before the Scary House's owner could lock us up like Hansel and Gretel. (I swore that I'd seen a bread-crumb trail leading to the playhouse.)

Just as scary as encountering a kid-eating witch was the prospect of another *Arachnophobia* situation ahead in the tunnel. And while I was not majorly worried about spiders, I was becoming less confident about our path with each step deeper into the darkness.

"Hold on, guys," I said. "I need to check the map to figure out where we are."

I flipped the map.

I rotated the map.

I shook the map.

No matter what I did, I couldn't make heads or tails of it.

"Are we there yet?" Diana whined in a muffled voice.

"What? I can't understand you with that thing over your mouth," I said.

Following the cobweb incident, Diana decided that spiders outranked bats in the hierarchy of spooky things in the dark, and she'd repositioned the scarf on her head. It now covered her nose and mouth, which made Diana look like she was about to rob a bank in the Wild West.

"Are we running out of oxygen down here?" she asked. "I think we're running out of air."

Johnny groaned. "We are not running out of air. I already told you three times."

"You could breathe better if you took that thingamajig off your face," Candice said.

"And have a spider crawl into my mouth? I don't think so."

"Diana, I think it is really nice that you're gonna let a bat live in your hair now," Bobby kidded.

"It's not funny! I only have one bandanna," she said, covering her exposed head with her hands.

"I'll be sure to direct any bats right over to you."

"Bobby!"

"I'll tell them to be on the lookout for the neon-green welcome sign on your face."

"*Bobby!* Cut it out!"

The friendly teasing made me giggle—until a drop of something fell onto my nose. I froze in my tracks, begging for it not to be bat pee. I slowly looked above my head to find the source of the mystery liquid. My eyes went up higher . . . and higher . . . until . . . I saw . . . nothing.

Whew!

Nothing was lurking in the shadows except for the same wire along the ceiling that Tommy had spotted earlier. Never had I been so happy to assume that I was the victim of a stalagmite or stalactite or whatever the thing was called that dripped from the top of caves.

I returned my attention to the map with its windy route to the *X* and the buried treasure. We obviously had been advancing toward the loot, but it was nearly impossible to have a sense of direction while underground, in the dark, and running from monster rats.

"What does it say?" Tommy asked me.

I wasn't sure of our location, but I decided to read another hint out loud even if I didn't know how close we were to it. "The next clue says, 'Fifty paces until the pot of gold.'"

"All right! We're almost there!" he cheered.

"After we save FDR, I am going to buy so many video games with the extra money we find," Bobby said. "And Knee-Slappers and Flimflams. I might even buy a whole candy store."

"I want a pair of long-range Ace Adventure 500 walkie-talkies," Johnny said. "And I want a boat and an RV for camping trips."

"You can't even drive," Candice said.

"I can drive in five years."

"In *1998*. There might be flying cars by 1998, and then you'll be stuck with some old RV that only works on the ground."

"The ground is where the camping is!"

"Well, I'm going to buy the new Roaring Rucksack squirt gun," Tommy said.

"The MegaBoost 2000? Me too!" Gina said. "And I want to get a lifetime subscription to *Duende Teen*."

"Becky, how far is it after the fifty paces?" Bobby asked.

I flipped the map one more time and pretended to understand it. "It's hard to tell exactly, but I think we're halfway there."

Diana looked over her shoulder. "We have to move. That thing is gaining on us."

"Don't worry. I have plenty more Hullabaloos," Gina said.

Johnny held out his hand. "Can I have one? I'm hungry."

"No!" Diana quickly jumped between the two of them. "No one can eat any Hullabaloos. We need to save them to get past the creature."

"Hey, look at that—a light bulb." Bobby shined his McNutt Lights on the ceiling, and sure enough, there was an oldfangled glass bulb hanging from the mystery cable.

And another one a few feet away.

And another after that.

"Electricity! The wire is electricity," Diana said with the type of wonder normally reserved for the dessert section of an all-you-can-eat buffet.

"There's the light switch," Tommy declared. He rushed over to the little toggle and flipped it.

Instantly, a comforting light illuminated the entire tunnel, and it was as if Thomas Edison himself had lifted a weight from my shoulders. I sighed in relief as my eyes adjusted to the soft, dim glow.

The collective feeling of calm lasted about one second until exploding light bulbs filled the tunnel with shards of glass.

"Booby trap!" Bobby yelled.

We screamed and huddled together with our arms covering our faces.

"I knew it! There is a curse!" Diana shrieked.

"Goblin be gone!" Gina shouted. "Be gone goblin!"

"We come in peace!" Candice said.

The final light bulb blew up right above us, and we were plunged into silent darkness.

"Are we booby-trapped?" Diana whispered.

Johnny aimed his flashlight at the ceiling. "It wasn't a booby trap. The wire is wet from condensation."

"Must have shorted out the lights," I said.

"False alarm on the booby trap," Bobby said.

"It wasn't the water," Tommy said. He was busy examining the fragments on the ground with his magnifying glass. "I think there was a power surge when I turned on the lights. One hundred twenty volts of modern electricity surging through bulbs from olden times and *bang!*"

"Cool!" Bobby kneeled next to his brother. "You and I should do exploding lights at the old cabin this summer with the cousins."

"The bits left on the ceiling won't burst into flames, will they?" Diana asked, studying the shattered remains above us.

Tommy walked back to the switch and flicked it back and forth. "Nope. They're dead as a doornail."

"Enough about the lights. Where is the bicycle?" Candice wildly swept her flashlight back and forth across the tunnel. "I swear I saw a bicycle!"

"OK, yeah, sure, you saw a bike down here," Johnny said, rolling his eyes. "And I saw a big-screen TV."

"Ooh, I want to buy a big-screen TV too!" Gina said. "I'm adding that to my list. A squirt gun, a lifetime subscription to *Duende Teen*, and a big-screen TV."

"Stop goofing around, guys," I said. "Fifty more paces to—"

"There it is!" Candice ran to a muddy old-fashioned bicycle that leaned against the side of the tunnel. A cart with wheels was attached to the back.

"Holy cow, she did find a bike!" Johnny said.

We all sprinted to Candice and the mysterious two-wheeler.

"I want to ride it," Gina said.

"Dibs!" Tommy shouted as he pushed Gina out of the way. "I get to ride it first! She didn't call dibs. I get to ride it!"

"No one is riding it," Candice said.

"But I called first dibs!"

"The tires are flat," she said. "And it's covered in cobwebs."

Johnny peered into the cart. "Whatever the opposite of treasure is, that's what we found. This thing is filled with the same textbook boxes that are in the secret room."

"Man, how many dopey math books does a person need?" Tommy asked. "I don't even need *one*."

"Johnny and Tommy, come help me look for booby traps," Bobby said. "I have to clear this area."

After Johnny wandered away with the McNutts, I moved over to where he'd been standing. I opened the two cruddy boxes—identical to the ones upstairs labeled ELEMENTARY MATHEMATICS—that were sitting inside the cart.

I was flabbergasted to find that they did not contain books of multiplication tables.

CHAPTER FIFTEEN

X Marks the Spot

▼ ▲ ▼ ▲ ▼

"*Bottles*. Both boxes are filled with lousy gin bottles." I glared disappointedly at the junky find in the cart.

"What's gin?" Candice asked.

"It's alcohol that old people drank during Prohibition," I said.

"And they drank it out of bathtubs," Diana added. "Or they made it in bathtubs. Something to do with bathtubs because Miss Warren always called it bathtub gin during Lucky's Loot."

Candice grimaced. "Ick! Grown-ups eat such gross things."

"Is gin worth a lot?" Gina asked. "We could sell these at Senior Keno Night at the library. I always make a ton of money when I sell cookies at Senior Keno. That's how I bought a dozen neon tetras for my aquarium."

I began inspecting the filthy bottles. "I dunno, there aren't any price—aw, nuts! Every single one of these is empty."

"They must be leftover garbage from Lucky's bootlegging," Candice said. She pulled a bottle out of the box and dusted off the label. "Bummer, they aren't deposit bottles. There goes a couple of bucks."

"Guys, come here!" Tommy yelled. "Johnny and I found a desk!"

The girls and I scurried over to Tommy, who was standing next to a large wooden desk by the wall. Magazines, fountain pens, a jar of darts, and a 1933 high school football schedule littered the surface.

"It's locked," Johnny said. He was kneeling on the ground, eye to eye with the keyhole in the center drawer. Holding out his hand he asked, "Becky, can I have your hairpin?"

"I don't have a hairpin. This is a barrette." I pointed to the rhinestone clip holding back my unruly bangs.

"That's not going to work. It's gotta be a hairpin." Johnny turned toward Gina, Candice, and Diana. "Someone give me a hairpin. I need it to pick the lock."

"Is a hairpin the same as a bobby pin?" Gina asked.

"I think so," Diana said.

"Nah, they must be different," Candice said, "because I've never heard anybody ask for a bobby pin to pick a lock. They always ask for hairpins in movies."

"Hey, I don't know all the names of stuff girls wear in their hair," Johnny said. "If you don't have a hairpin, then give me a bobby pin."

"What kind of pen do you want?" Bobby asked. He'd just returned from booby trap patrol. "I have ballpoint, felt-tip, fountain, roller—"

"I don't want a pen. I want a *pin*, a bobby *pin*."

"And I said, I have ballpoint, felt-tip—"

"Bobby, I don't want a pen!"

"Then stop asking me for one."

"For the love of Dick Tracy, someone give me a bobby pin or hairpin or whatever it's called so I can pick this lock!"

"It's pretty obvious that none of us are wearing either," Gina said.

Johnny began pounding on the wood in an attempt to dislodge the drawer. "How am I supposed to get this open?"

"We smash it with the chair," Tommy said. He lunged for his preferred tool for opening things, but I grabbed it before he did.

"Hold on! Maybe there's a secret button or something that opens the drawers." I pulled the chair back and crawled under the desk with my flashlight. But I shouldn't have been so eager to investigate because there were a million vile cobwebs.

"Spiders, spiders, spiders!" I squealed as I shot up and scooted away from the desk. Clawing at the clingy crud stuck to my face and T-shirt, I bent over and shook my hair upside down. "Are there any on me?"

Diana, keeping a safe distance, pointed her flashlight at my head. "Not that I can see."

I shivered. "Yech."

"Bet you wish you had one of these covering your nose and mouth," Diana said, tightening the knot on her kerchief. "Who's laughing about spiders now?"

"I never made fun of your scarf," I said while fixing the sparkly barrette that I'd knocked out of place. "That was Tommy and Johnny and—"

"It's open!" Candice proclaimed. She pointed to the unlocked desk drawer.

"How did you do that?" I asked.

"My little cousin got trapped in our bathroom last month, so my dad popped the lock with a meat thermometer." Candice held up a dart that she'd plucked from the cup on the desk. "This is pretty much the same thing."

I tingled at the prospect of digging through the desk and finding old-timey treasures like a rookie Babe Ruth baseball card. I didn't know much about the sport, but I'd heard of Babe Ruth since he was famous enough to have his picture hanging inside Betty's Burger Beanery. I also knew that rookie cards were the most valuable because Johnny once told me that I should never trade one if I was lucky enough to receive one. And I had received loads of different cards thanks to the firefighters in my town.

Ever since I could remember, those women and men had carried special department-branded baseball cards to hand out to kids—for free! Whenever anyone in the Sherlock Pines Gang spotted a fire truck (usually near a safety presentation at school or the mall or Delta Sue's Dime Store), we flagged it down with the hope of snagging the best new players. The first question I always asked the firefighters was, "Do you have any rookies?" And they always replied, "Gee, I don't know, but I have a good feeling about this one! Stay in school and don't play with matches." Then I'd run home, look up the player in my mom's sports almanac, and get bummed out at my dud card.

But maybe I was finally going to get lucky! I figured that any boring baseball card purchased in the 1920s and 1930s had to be a collectible in the 1990s. And I was certain that bootleggers were baseball fans because I didn't know what else they would have done for fun before TV or video games.

Looking into the open center drawer, I spotted two well-used hardcover notebooks labeled LEDGER. I pushed them aside as I searched and failed to find baseball cards or any other valuable stuff. Disappointed, I removed one of the ledgers as a consolation prize. While skimming it, I noticed that it contained many similar notations.

"Huh . . . this is full of handwritten lists of people and money," I said.

Gina leaned over my shoulder. "It looks like the accounting book that Scrooge wrote in while he yelled at Bob Cratchit."

"Then those are probably Lucky's bootlegging customers," Diana said.

I turned the page. "You're right! Here's list of gin bottles hidden inside hay bales. They were all delivered to Declan Doyle's farm."

Entries detailing the illegal bootlegging activities of Lucky Killarney filled the pages of the musty book. Client after client such as the coffeehouse, the flower shop, and the sheriff's department was listed in the ledger, along with the alcohol they ordered and how much money they owed. The log was written in that perfect kind of swirly penmanship that grandparents use.

"Same type of entries in this book except that they're all for a single client: McCoy Dance Hall," Johnny said while reading the second ledger. "The dates in here go through 1933."

"That's when Prohibition ended, right?" Candice asked.

"Yep," Diana said, "the Twenty-first Amendment was ratified in December 1933."

"But that doesn't make any sense," I said. "Lucky wrote the treasure map and disappeared in 1932."

Unbothered by the date discrepancy, Johnny laughed as he focused on what he thought was the most important thing about his ledger. "Lucky sure wrote like a girl—look." He showed me a page that listed the speakeasy's booze orders for April 1928. The cursive handwriting didn't match anything that I had seen in my notebook, but it seemed startlingly familiar.

And then it hit me.

"That's the same handwriting as the grade book in the secret room!" I said. "I'm sure the weird letter *A* used to write *April* matches the A grades in Mrs. Doyle's book upstairs."

"Wow, so the rumors are true! Mrs. Doyle really did help run the speakeasy," Johnny said.

I nodded. "Which means this desk must have been their top secret office. They'd sneak in here using the hidden passage at school."

"That was a really smart idea," Candice said. "No one would ever think that a teacher was in Lucky Killarney's bootlegging gang."

"Boy, teachers can sure get away with anything," Johnny said.

His comment got me thinking about what Mrs. Andrews really did during all those weekends when she said she was trapped at weddings across the country. I started to question whether there could possibly be that many weddings a person had to attend on a weekly basis. In my entire life, I'd only been to one wedding and that was because my dad was a groomsman.

"This desk is a bust for treasure," Tommy announced. He and Bobby had been digging through the remaining drawers while Johnny and I reviewed the ledgers with Gina, Candice, and Diana.

"No secret compartments. No diamonds. No gold," Bobby said. "It's as empty as my piggy bank after a trip to Otter's Joke Shop."

"Yeah, we only found cigars, paper clips, and an old baseball," Tommy said.

"Can I have the baseball?" Gina asked. "I lost mine in Scotland Yard last week. I think a Meschino swiped it."

Tommy tossed the ball between his hands. "Maybe, but you didn't say the magic word."

"Please."

"Please what?"

Annoyed, Gina dramatically rolled her eyes. "Please, Captain Tommy, Ruler of Rad and Lord of the Land, can I have the baseball?"

"That's better," he said and threw the grimy ball to her.

Bobby slammed a drawer shut. "What a bunch of garbage! Some *X* marks the spot."

"Because this isn't where *X* marks the spot," I said. "We still had fifty paces to go when the lights exploded. That was the last step I read on the map."

"It's the cuckoo clock," Diana said.

I was confused. "I don't remember that clue. Where'd it say that on the map?"

"No, *the* cuckoo clock! The missing cuckoo clock from FDR!" She pointed her flashlight to the world's most legendary clock hanging a few feet away from the desk.

"Whoa!" Candice said.

"Holy moly!" I said.

Diana dragged the desk chair to the clock and climbed up for a better look. "It's the same weird bald eagle and pinecone chains all right. But the wood is covered in tiny holes. Must be termites."

"Take it down so we can see it," Johnny said.

"Are you crazy? I'm not touching it if it's full of termites," Diana said, hopping off the chair.

141

"Never fear, the bug expert is here!" Bobby clambered up the chair to give his specialist opinion about the marks on the clock. "These aren't bug holes."

"Please don't tell me that they're from bat teeth," I said.

"Bats don't eat wood, Becky," Candice said. She raised her arms like wings and stumbled toward me. *"They vant to drink your blood!"*

I swatted her arms out of my face. "That's not funny, Candice! You saw how all those vampire bats were sucking blood on the zoo field trip."

"Can someone give me one of those darts on the desk?" Bobby asked. He took one from Diana and fitted it neatly into a hole on the cuckoo clock. "Just like I thought. Someone was using this for dart practice."

"I used to do the same thing with *Dick Tracy* trading cards," Johnny said. "Had all the bad guys taped in a lineup on my bedroom wall." He mimed his throwing technique for us. "Pfft! Pfft! Pfft!"

"That's such a mean thing, stealing Mr. Grundy's clock and throwing darts at it all day long," Diana said.

"They say everyone hated it since it made so much noise," Gina said as she twirled the pinecone weights dangling under the clock.

"But why would Lucky steal it?" Diana asked. "What did it ever do to him?"

Gina shrugged. "Gangsters steal stuff. That's why they have getaway cars."

"I bet it was Mrs. Doyle," I said. "We know she was down here 'cause of the ledgers. And she would have been the only one in the gang who was forced to listen to it cuckoo all day."

Candice chuckled. "So she hid it right under Mr. Grundy's nose and used it for dart practice. That's pretty rad."

"Bobby, turn it on. I wanna hear it," Johnny said.

"I'm trying," he said, inspecting the clock with his McNutt Lights, "but I can't find the power button."

"Don't turn it on! It might explode from another power surge," Diana said.

"We should take it with us," I suggested. "I bet there is a lot of reward money. It's the most famous missing thing in town."

Bobby unhooked the large clock and nearly collapsed under the unexpected weight. "Oof, can someone give me a hand? These metal pinecones weigh a ton."

Tommy helped his brother maneuver the valuable item safely to the ground. "Jeez, I'm glad they no longer make clocks with all this heavy stuff hanging on chains. What a stupid decoration."

"I can carry it in my bag, but I have to make room," Bobby said. He jumped off the chair and started emptying items from his backpack. "I need people to take my shovel . . . and my duct tape . . . and my hammer . . ."

"I have room for the hammer," Johnny said, grabbing the tool. "Ooh, this is a nice one! Becky, look how good this would be for tapping trees."

"Yeah, it would be," I said, sighing. "But we can't try to make syrup anymore. My dad flipped out when he saw all the nails you and I hammered into the sugar maple."

Diana put two rolls of duct tape into her bag. "Seems like overkill on the tape, Bobby. Did you really need to bring five rolls?"

He looked at Diana as if she'd just asked him if the earth rotated around the sun. "You can never have enough duct tape in an exploring situation."

"I've never carried duct tape on any of our adventures."

"And that is why you're not a booby trap expert like me." Bobby held up another item. "Who has room for my PKE meter?"

"I can squeeze it into my bag," I said, taking the *Ghostbusters* toy.

Candice paused while jamming Bobby's bag of pens into her backpack. "What's that sound?"

"It's my stomach," Johnny said. "I'm starving to death, but *someone* won't let me eat a Hullabaloo."

"Because we need them for the creature," Diana said.

"No . . . it's not Johnny's stomach," Candice said. "It's something else farther down the tunnel."

I strained to listen. "I hear it too." I couldn't put my finger on the type of noise, but there was definitely a faint muffled sound in the distance.

Petrified, Diana whispered, "Gina, get a Hullabaloo!"

"But I don't hear anything."

"Neither do I," Bobby said. He hoisted his hulking backpack over his shoulders. "All right, I'm ready."

I signaled for the Sherlock Pines Gang to follow me deeper into the pitch-black tunnel. "OK, fifty paces, everybody."

I'd only counted off a few steps before the mysterious noise intensified.

"Now I hear it," Johnny said.

"Yeah, it's kind of a thumping sound," Tommy said. "Like Frankenstein skipping down a hallway."

"What if it's something way worse than the giant rat?" Diana whimpered.

"It wasn't a rat. It was an opossum," Gina said.

"Whatever it was—McNutts, you should be in the front," Diana said. She hastily positioned herself at the back of the group. "Your hands are free to punch whatever is down there."

"Diana, it's fine," I said. "It's probably the wind making a weird noise like when you blow across the top of a . . ."

"What? What is it? Why did we stop walking?" she asked.

"It's the end," I said, flummoxed. "We're at the end."

"Oh man! This is it!" Diana said.

"Of the *tunnel*, Diana! We are at the end of the tunnel." I gestured to the dirt and wood in front of me. "See?"

"Is this the *X*?" Bobby asked frantically. "Who has my shovel? I need my shovel!"

I aimed my flashlight at the wall and saw a handle. "It's a door."

"Is there an *X* on it? Someone give me my shovel!"

Candice pressed her ear against the wood and listened. "The noise is louder behind this, but I still can't make it out. It's something like . . . like . . . 'The Loco-Motion'?"

"Oh my gosh! Guys, I remember a veejay said the singer of that song is Australian! Maybe we tunneled so far down that we actually reached Australia!" Gina said giddily. "Do any of you speak Australian? The only word I know is *g'day*, which means 'hello.'"

"Australia? C'mon, Gina," Johnny said, "your hat is still on your head, so we're obviously not upside down."

Diana nervously hovered behind me. "Becky, please, *please* tell me that thing is not rusted shut."

I grasped the metal handle and pushed. It shifted upward with a clank, and I felt the heavy door move. "Nope, it's open." I steadied my nerves. "OK. We go on three. One, two—"

"Wait!" Tommy squeezed his way over to me, brandishing one can of Zany Ribbons party string in each hand. "Just in case."

I gave a thumbs-up and positioned myself so that he could stand next to me as I shoved open the door. "One, two, *three*!"

CHAPTER SIXTEEN

The Party from H-E-Double-Hockey-Sticks

▼ ▲ ▼ ▲ ▼

"En garde! It's the Sherlock Pines Gang!" Tommy bellowed as he and I charged into a bright room amid a neon tornado of Zany Ribbons. Between the spray streamer and the glare, I could barely see what was in front of me.

But the room was chock-full of people. And it was really noisy.

"I *do* hear 'The Loco-Motion'!" Candice said from behind me. "Are we at the roller rink?"

Squinting from the blinding light, I brushed strands of Zany Ribbons out of my eyes and tried to scan the area. "I don't think so, but I do smell—"

"Hot dogs!" Johnny said, shoving his way past me. "Where are they? I'm starving!"

"Johnny!" a familiar voice shouted from deep within the crowd.

Moments later, Jenny Juneau, Johnny's fourteen-year-old sister, inexplicably emerged from the throng alongside Gina's brother, Curtis. "Johnny, what on earth are you doing behind there?" she demanded. "You totally broke the Sherlock painting off the wall."

147

I turned around and sure enough—the door I just walked through had a huge painting of Sherlock Holmes on this side.

A very familiar painting of Sherlock Holmes.

A very familiar painting of Sherlock Holmes that I knew hung inside the picnic pavilion.

"Oh no," I mumbled, feeling like the stuffing had been knocked out of me. Crushed, I shared the depressing news with everyone still in the tunnel. "We're in Scotland Yard."

"England? I can't believe we tunneled to England!" Gina said. "Do any of you speak English? I know the word *supercalifragi—*"

"The *picnic pavilion*, Gina. We're in the Scotland Yard picnic pavilion," I said.

My brain struggled to wrap itself around the situation. Of all the picnic pavilions in all the towns in all the world, I had to walk through a secret passage, outrun an opossum rat, and escape exploding lights only to end up back inside the one that was hosting Sean Meschino's miserable party.

"Move it, Becky! You're blocking the exit!" Diana bulldozed me out of the way, eagerly emerging from the tunnel. Candice, Gina, and Bobby followed close behind her.

Jenny was dumbfounded by the parade of sixth graders climbing out from behind Sherlock. "It's like a clown car of dorks."

"With their bank-robbing friend, Jesse James," Curtis said, eyeing Diana's neon-green spider shield.

Diana ripped the bandanna off her face the second she saw her crush. "Hi, Curtis! How are you?"

"Hey," he said flatly. "You have something stuck on your head."

His response absolutely delighted Diana since he'd never said more than "hey" to her during her whole life. "Thank you for letting me know that I had something in my hair, Curtis. You are so nice," she said, coolly removing a cobwebby leaf from her messy hair. "You look really good in that tie-dye shirt, by the way."

Taking no notice of Diana's compliment, Curtis sized up our ragtag group. "You guys reek like gym socks."

"Phew, no kidding!" Jenny pinched her nose and glared at her brother. "Why are you and your weird little friends crawling out of walls?"

Johnny excitedly began telling the story of our adventure. "We were in the teachers' lounge—"

"The bookcase moved!" Candice said.

"Then we battled a gigantic rat," Diana said.

"Bobby and I made these McNutt Lights to hunt for the treasure," Tommy said, proudly pointing to the Zany Ribbons–covered contraption on his head.

"Lucky Killarney's treasure," Bobby added.

"We followed those McNutt Lights so far down that we almost reached Australia," Gina said. "I swear!"

Jenny exchanged a look with Curtis before sneering at us. "Man, you guys are screwier than I thought if you randomly followed the McNutts down some stinky hole."

"No, it's true. We *were* on a treasure hunt," I said as I unzipped my bag. "I'll show you the map."

"And thanks to my expertise," Bobby bragged to the Big Kids, "we escaped every booby trap."

"There weren't any booby traps," Candice said.

He spun around and came face-to-face with her. "Because we escaped them."

"You can't escape something that doesn't exist. That's like saying we escaped all the ghosts in the tunnel."

"We did escape all the ghosts! My PKE meter didn't go off once."

"Because it's not a real one! You made it out of tinfoil, pipe cleaners, and a macaroni box."

Bobby snorted. "Shows what you know about ectoplasm and tinfoil."

I opened the map for Jenny, and I traced our path with my finger. "Look—we found two secret passages and a secret room at FDR. They led to this underground tunnel. We walked down the whole thing and ended up here through the Sherlock painting."

Jenny quietly stared at the paper in my hands. I assumed she was speechless at the sight of the amazing discovery. It was surely the first treasure map that Jenny Juneau had laid eyes upon, and she needed time to take it in.

Then she started laughing.

It was one of those hard, mean laughs intended to make someone feel bad, which in this case was me and the Sherlock Pines Gang. Johnny's sister had obviously been spending too much time hanging out with too many Meschinos.

"*This* is your treasure map?" Jenny said, snatching the document from me.

"Careful! That's over fifty years old!" I said.

"More like five years old," she said. "This is Will's map."

"Will? I thought Lucky's real name was Nicky," Diana said.

"Will *Meschino*, you doofus. From my grade," Jenny replied.

"For real?" Curtis leaned over Jenny's shoulder. "Ha, I totally remember when Will drew this!"

"He didn't draw it. That's a real treasure map," Tommy said.

"Yeah, a *real* treasure map," Johnny said. "You don't know what you're talking about, Jenny."

"Will!" Curtis shouted into the crowd. "Come over here!"

Fourteen-year-old Will Meschino muscled his way through partygoers while stuffing a hot dog into his mouth. As soon as he arrived at our group, a blob of ketchup, which he ignored, dripped onto his Beavis and Butt-head T-shirt. "What's up?"

Curtis held the map in front of Will's face. "Remember drawing this in third grade?"

"No way, dude! Where did you find that?"

"These dorks had it and were playing treasure hunt with it."

"You're the dork, Curtis!" Gina said. "Now give that back to Becky, or I'm telling Mom."

"Shut up, Gina," he said, pushing her away.

"The boneheads thought my homework was a treasure map?" Will cackled in the same crude manner as the cartoon characters on his T-shirt. "That is the most hilarious thing I've ever heard. Sean is gonna bust a gut when he gets here."

I rolled my eyes. Of course Sean Meschino was still not at his own party.

Will jammed the rest of the hot dog into his mouth. "How'd the geeks get it out of my permanent record?"

My eyeballs immediately stopped rolling.

Slipping back into panic mode, Diana blurted out, "We didn't take your permanent record! Why would we take permanent records? We don't have any permanent records!"

Candice elbowed her. *"Ixnay!"*

Will licked his fingers and took the map from Curtis. "Mrs. Parish put this in my file when she suspended me for making it for Lucky's Loot."

"Lucky's Loot?" Each word tumbled out of my mouth with the deadweight of ten tons.

Gina gasped. "Oh no! Becky, if that's true, I think I know what happened."

"It's not true," I assured her. "They're just messing with us."

"But in alphabetical order, Will's file—"

"Will's file hasn't been at FDR since he went to middle school," I said. "So even if he did draw the map—which he didn't—it wouldn't have gotten mixed up with Bobby's folder last week."

"Because it was already mixed up! Mrs. Parish accidentally stuck the map in Bobby *McNutt's* permanent record instead of Will *Meschino's* back when we were in kindergarten and he was in third grade!"

"Whoa," Johnny said.

"Whoa is right!" Candice said. "Talk about a screwup."

"Yep," Gina said. "Which means Becky didn't grab the map off the desk in the secret room like we thought she did. It was in Bobby's file the whole time."

Bobby, being a McNutt, was more interested in Will's shenanigans rather than Gina's ridiculous theory. "A suspension? What did you do, Will?"

"I lit the map on fire in class," he said. "You know, to burn the edges and make it look old. Mrs. Parish and Miss Warren did not appreciate my attention to detail."

"Well, these dummies did!" Jenny said, laughing up a storm. "They followed it because they thought it was a real treasure map."

Will fake coughed, *"Nerds!"*

I'd had enough. "Give it to me," I said, trying to retrieve the map from one of the meanest Big Kids in Sherlock Pines.

But Will held it over my head in a move straight out of the Meschino playbook. "Why are you jumping, Becky? Are you trying to give me a kiss? Tricia told me how much you wanted to kiss me."

"Give it back! That is a real treasure map, and it's mine."

"Oh yeah? I don't think real treasure maps look like this." Will began folding the paper in thirds.

"Stop it! You're gonna tear it!"

Ignoring me, he continued overlapping the document like a *MAD Magazine* fold-in until it was transformed into a naughty sketch of something that boys liked to draw on bathroom walls.

Bobby, Tommy, Johnny, Curtis, and Jenny expressed their hearty appreciation of such a finely crafted drawing that was going to be turned in as homework.

"That's amazing, Will!" Bobby said.

"Mrs. Parish didn't even know that was on there!" Tommy giggled. "Teachers are so stupid."

The evidence that a Meschino had drawn the map was now piled sky-high. Gina was right, and I had to accept the truth. "Lucky Killarney didn't draw this."

"No, duh, Becky. You're a real rocket scientist," Will said.

Everything had gone higgledy-piggledy with the crazy revelation that Will Meschino had drawn the treasure map. The treasure map that had somehow just guided me through several very real hidden passages. "But . . . but we followed the map into a tunnel."

"It smells like you followed these McNutt Lights into a sewer," Jenny said as she flicked her finger on Tommy's prized invention.

"Hands off!" he said, pushing away Jenny's arm. "That's personal property."

I stared at Will. "When did you find out about the secret room in the teachers' lounge?"

"What secret room?"

"At the start of the tunnel on the map you drew. The start of Lucky Killarney's tunnel."

"I think you're one slice short of a whole pizza, Becky."

"Wait a minute, she's right!" Johnny said. "Forget about the fact that Will drew the map. There's still a hidden passage in the—"

Before Johnny was able to explain the Sherlock Pines Gang's discovery, another Meschino interrupted him.

"There she is, Mrs. Parish!" Tricia Meschino screamed.

She marched over to me, dragging the principal with her. Mrs. Parish's German shepherd, Elvis, trotted alongside his master and made occasional pit stops to inhale the trail of hot dog crumbs dropped by Will.

I shuddered. Seeing a principal outside of school was one of the worst things a kid could experience, especially if that principal was Mrs. Parish.

Tricia launched straight into tattling. "Becky Dulles was sneaking around in the teachers' lounge during lunch today. I bet all her friends were in there too."

Rachel, Tricia's matching-headband-wearing lackey, popped out from behind her friend. "They were all sneaking around in the teachers' lounge, Mrs. Parish!"

"Becky, you know students aren't allowed inside that room," the principal said. "What were you doing in there?"

I stared at her as a fury I had never known bubbled up inside me.

I was mad at Mrs. Parish, at Tricia, and at Will's stupid map.

I was mad that I didn't find the treasure.

I was mad that I didn't save FDR.

Most of all, I was mad that I'd let everyone down.

"I asked you a question, Becky. What were you doing in the teachers' lounge?"

The churning rage suddenly exploded out of me like a verbal version of the Memorial Day Vomiting. "What do you care, Mrs. Parish? You're not the boss of me anymore!"

"Young lady, I made it quite clear that just because Franklin D. Roosevelt Elementary is closing—"

"Exactly! You're not my principal. You can't do anything to me." I shocked myself with the language I was using to speak to Mrs. Parish. I sounded like a McNutt. Maybe worse! But I couldn't stop.

I had never felt more alive in my whole life!

"Oh no? In case you forgot, I can still add this misbehavior to your permanent record," Mrs. Parish said.

"Ha!" I snorted. "Good luck with that!"

"Tell me what you were doing in the teachers' lounge."

Exasperated, I spilled the beans. "We were looking for Lucky Killarney's treasure. There. That's it. Are you happy now?"

Mrs. Parish crossed her arms in a really annoying way. "Becky, I know that you know those Lucky's Loot treasure hunts are no more real than hunting for the Fountain of Youth. And it's certainly no excuse to go snooping in the teachers' lounge."

"It's true, Mrs. Parish!" Diana said. "We were on a real treasure hunt."

"We just didn't find any treasure," Johnny said.

Then it hit me like a dodgeball in gym class.

"Wait, we did!" I said. "The clock—Mrs. Parish, we found the cuckoo clock!"

"I'll show you! I'm the one who spotted it on the wall," Diana said as she ran over to Bobby.

She swiftly lifted the cuckoo clock from the safety of his backpack, but the tangled iron chains were wrapped around a spare flashlight at the bottom of the bag. Unprepared for the heavy drag, Diana lost control and the bulky clock slipped through her fingers.

The dark, brittle wood shattered into a million pieces when it hit the floor.

CHAPTER SEVENTEEN

A Humpty-Dumpty Situation

▼ ▲ ▼ ▲ ▼

I couldn't believe it.

I couldn't believe it even as I watched the wood disintegrate in front of me.

I couldn't believe that Diana had smashed the cuckoo clock—the priceless FDR cuckoo clock—into one zillion little pieces.

"No!" I cried.

"I'm sorry! I'm sorry! I'm sorry!" Diana immediately collapsed to her knees and began gathering the fragments that were strewn across the picnic pavilion. "We can glue it back together. I'm sure we can."

"Do we still get a reward, Mrs. Parish?" Bobby asked.

"Reward? There's no reward for anything," she said.

"Because Dull Becky Dulles and her friends stole it!" Tricia argued. "You can't reward them for something they stole."

The principal eyeballed each member of the Sherlock Pines Gang. "Explain to me what this is. Right now."

"We told you. It's Mr. Grundy's clock that we found in the tunnel," Johnny said.

"Don't you recognize it?" Gina said. "I mean, it's mostly in smithereens now, but . . ."

"Even if it is in smithereens, I bet there's a reward for finding it," Tommy said. "You should check, Mrs. Parish."

Tricia fumed at the McNutts. "You can't get a reward for something that you destroyed."

"Yeah, dummies. You destroyed it," Rachel chimed in.

"Everything is fine! I just need a little glue," Diana said. "My mom has some really good glue."

"Diana, I think this is a Humpty-Dumpty situation," Candice said.

"I can glue this back together again!" she snapped.

"I'm going to ask one last time, and I want the truth," Mrs. Parish said. "Who did you take this from?"

"Argh, you never listen! We didn't take it from anyone!" I picked up the wooden bald eagle from the floor and showed it to her. "Look—same eagle wearing a top hat that's in Mr. Grundy's photo."

Mrs. Parish took the piece from me and stared at it. "I'll be darned. This *is* Mr. Grundy's cuckoo clock!"

"Told you so!" Bobby said. "Now about that reward."

The possibility of the Sherlock Pines Gang receiving any prize made Tricia see red. "You airheads are not getting a reward!"

"Yeah, airheads! No reward for you," Rachel said.

Mrs. Parish wheeled around. "Tricia and Rachel, mind your own business! This does not concern you."

Taken aback by an unexpected scolding from the principal, Tricia looked at her brother for backup. But Will's eyes were glued to the clock, and his ketchup-covered mouth hung open in silence.

"Let's go, Rachel. I want cake," Tricia said and stormed off with her flunky in tow.

Mrs. Parish circled back to us. "Where did you say you found this clock?"

"The tunnel!" the McNutts shouted.

"It's right behind Sherlock Holmes," Johnny said.

"Come on, Mrs. Parish," Candice said. "We'll show you."

"It is really neat. Especially the exploding lights," Bobby said.

Gina started digging in her backpack. "You'll need a Hullabaloo to throw at the creature. It likes Surprise Party, but I don't have more of that flavor. Here's a Snow Day."

The principal took the Hullabaloo. "What creature?"

"I'll show you—come on!" Gina said. She and Candice grabbed Mrs. Parish's hands and pulled her toward the Sherlock painting.

Tommy sped to the tunnel entrance with his brother. "Bobby and I have to go in first so the McNutt Lights show the way."

A gawking mob of party attendees followed the gang, which left Diana and me sitting alone with the cuckoo clock catastrophe.

My eyes filled with tears as I gazed blankly at the wreckage. Not even *The Bodyguard* soundtrack blaring from the boom box could lift my spirits.

Diana seemed to be on the verge of crying too. "I'm so sorry, Becky. I ruined everything. I understand if you never, ever forgive me for the rest of my whole entire life."

I started sliding the pieces of wood around on the floor because I knew I'd start bawling if I spoke.

"I ruined all your plans," she continued. "We're definitely not getting the clock reward. And now we have to go to different schools. Which means we're not going to high school together. And it stinks."

"Yeah. It stinks."

"We can glue it back together," Diana said, although she sounded like she no longer believed the words coming out of her mouth.

"You know, we weren't on a treasure hunt for the clock."

"Which we can glue."

"It was kind of a bonus that you found it," I said. "Lucky's treasure is still out there, and we have the whole summer to look for it before we go back to school."

"I wish we were going to the same school."

"Me too."

I leaned over to hug Diana, but a big, wet dog nose came between us. Elvis had apparently decided that it was the right time to investigate the wreckage for food crumbs.

"Ugh, Elvis, get out of here! Go find Mrs. Parish." As I pushed him away, something caught my eye in the rubble. I moved one of the metal pinecones and discovered a brown leather pouch that blended in with the mound of sharp, splintery wood.

Diana and I stared at each other, bursting with excitement. It felt just like the time we discovered my dad's stash of leftover Halloween candy hidden behind five cans of lima beans.

I picked up the hefty sack and brushed away the grime. A small brand was burned into the leather.

"It's a lucky clover," Diana whispered.

My hands trembled as I opened it.

"Oh my gosh," Diana said as she watched gold coins spill into my hands. "Oh my gosh!"

"Wait—it might be more Fullalove candy."

Diana took a coin out of my hand and scraped at the foil edge.

But there was no foil edge.

And there was no mark of Fullalove Confectioners.

There was only a lady in a dress on one side and a soaring bald eagle on the other side. The words *United States of America* ran across the top of the coin.

"Lucky's treasure?" I asked.

Diana nodded. "Lucky's treasure."

"Lucky's treasure!" I screamed. "Lucky's treasure!"

"We found Lucky Killarney's treasure!" Diana jumped up and down, waving the gold coin in the air.

▲ ▼ ▲

In the days following Diana's amazing, butterfingered discovery, everyone—including Mrs. Parish—hailed the Sherlock Pines Gang as heroes and bona fide real-life treasure hunters.

The month of June quickly became a blur of celebratory sparkling-apple-cider toasts and restaurant pizza from Viv's Pizza Place. No one threw a parade down Main Street for us, but we did get the front page of the *Tri-County Herald Star Telegram* with the headline: LOCAL KIDS DISCOVER MISSING GRUNDY CUCKOO CLOCK! AND GOLD!

The newspaper's team of investigative reporters determined that the secret room I found in the teachers' lounge was the beginning of the supply tunnel for the McCoy Dance Hall. With the tunnel's existence confirmed, the Tri-County Historical Society was finally able to prove how Lucky kept the speakeasy stocked with illegal booze for so many years.

According to the experts, Lucky regularly delivered alcohol, hidden inside hay bales, to Declan Doyle's farm. That was where Mrs. Doyle removed the full bottles and concealed them in empty textbook boxes. (A revelation that fueled additional questions and concerns of mine about what teachers did during weekends.) Safely tucked inside boring-looking containers, the bottles easily made their way into Liberty Elementary via Mrs. Doyle. She then carted the liquor through the underground passage directly into the speakeasy, where Lucky sold it for an enormous profit.

The secret route from Liberty to McCoy ensured that no one saw a single alcohol delivery to the speakeasy during Prohibition. Not even sharp-eyed Mrs. Grundy, Prohibition fan and McCoy dance teacher, ever witnessed the arrival of anything suspicious.

By the early 1930s, Lucky had accumulated so much gold from his statewide bootlegging scheme that he needed a safe spot to stash his loot. It had to be a place that was both dull and obvious. A place that no one would want to investigate.

A place such as the despised, hated, vile cuckoo clock.

Historians marveled at the selection of a location so perfect that not even Mrs. Doyle had a clue as to what was hidden inside the object she regularly used for dart practice. However, there was no hiding spot, no matter how perfect, that could outwit the teamwork and talent of the Sherlock Pines Gang.

The face value of Lucky's gold coins was twenty dollars each, but they were worth way more than that because of their connection to the famous gangster. Way, way more than that. The final value of the Saint-Gaudens double-eagle gold coins was a number with more zeros than I ever imagined was possible. The number was so big that my dad shook his head and said "Holy smoke" for three days straight every time he thought about it.

The school district, being the school district, immediately claimed ownership of the treasure on the grounds that it was literally in the ground under FDR. But Mrs. McNutt, being a fancy lawyer who ate Debonairs, argued our winning case of finders keepers.

The losers weepers then got real nosy about the disappearance of seven permanent records that, in their words, "suspiciously belonged to the kids who broke into the teachers' lounge." In a killer comeback, Mrs. McNutt told the school district that they themselves had lost the files because of their own sloppiness. It was case closed as soon as she suggested an audit of all their records. (Tommy told me that *audit* was one of the scariest words adults could hear, which was precisely why his mom had used it.)

After Mrs. McNutt's impressive victory, she followed instructions from the Sherlock Pines Gang to offer a large donation of gold to the school district—but only if they promised to use the money for three specific things: keeping FDR open, building monkey bars at Meadow View, and painting hopscotch courts at Lenah Higbee.

They promised. And the good news rapidly spread high and low across the Mom Network.

Eventually the brouhaha over Lucky's treasure died down as the summer temperature rose. It simply became too hot to discuss anything other than snow cones or ice cream, except for the occasional fight about a rock-paper-scissors game.

By the beginning of July, things felt like they were back to normal around the neighborhood. The birds sang, the bees buzzed, and the Sherlock Pines Gang was camped out 24-7 at Candice's pool.

CHAPTER EIGHTEEN

Sherlock Pines Gang Forever

▼ ▲ ▼ ▲ ▼

"Cannonball!"

I leaped from the diving board, tucked myself into a tight ball and plunged into the Cohens' swimming pool. Based upon the number of screams I heard as I sank into the water, I judged my cannonball form to be a perfect ten.

But Diana wasn't impressed, and she splashed water in my face when I surfaced next to her yellow inner tube. "Becky, you got my new magazine all wet!"

"I said *cannonball*."

The Law of Kids had clear rules regarding cannonball policy as it related to jumping into a crowded pool.

Rule number one stated: Do it and yell *cannonball*!

Rule number two stated: There are no more rules. Cannonball!

Therefore, I knew that Diana knew her complaints were no good, even though she continued to whine about it.

"You didn't give me time to get out of the way, so now my

Duende Teen is ruined. And there was a coupon in it for one free Ful-lalove candy. Any flavor!"

"Don't get all bent out of shape. It'll dry off," I said. "Besides, you shouldn't float around with a magazine in the deep end if you can't handle cannonballs."

"Cannonball!" Candice bellowed as she jumped into the pool, landing right next to us.

Diana wailed, "Argh, Candice! You did that on purpose!"

"I said *cannonball*," she giggled.

"Stop laughing! It's not funny!" In a huff, Diana put the magazine between her teeth and paddled to safety in the shallow end.

Candice swam over to me. "Becky, watch and tell me if I look dead when I do this." She took a deep breath and floated facedown with her arms dangling by her side. After ten seconds, she popped up and looked at me in earnest as she wiped water from her eyes. "Did I look dead? I've been practicing."

"I guess you did. Why do you want to look dead?"

"Because I want Lifeguard Tom Cruise to rescue me and give me mouth-to-mouth. He's gonna be the Wendy Peffercorn to my Squints. Just like in *The Sandlot*."

"But Wendy Peffercorn banned Squints from the pool after he fake drowned to kiss her," I said.

"That's a chance I'm willing to take."

"I'm not! She also banned Squints's friends from the pool. For life! I don't want next week to be our last trip to P. Tonnes."

Candice smiled. "I forget when we're going to P. Tonnes. Are we going to P. Tonnes after we drink a lot of pop?"

"I'm serious! Don't make the lifeguards angry."

"I'm sure we can still slip inside the water park if we're banned. If anyone can figure out a sneaky way to P. Tonnes, it's you—" Candice stopped talking to me as soon as she noticed a McNutt enter the pool area. "Tommy! Where have you been?"

"Have you seen Gina?" he asked.

I swiveled around in the water to look at Tommy. He was briskly lifting his feet up and down as he stood barefoot on the hot concrete.

"What's with all the dancing? You look like you are going to P. Tonnes," Candice said.

Tommy smirked. "I'm not going to P. Tonnes today. I'm going to P. Tonnes next week."

"You guys are so immature," Diana said. She was floating by the edge of the pool and drying her *Duende Teen* with a Miss Piggy beach towel.

"Well? Do you know where Gina is?" Tommy asked as he jumped around. "Hurry up and tell me. My feet are on fire."

Candice tried to suppress an exaggerated tone of voice as she answered. "No, no, I have no idea. Becky, do you know where Gina is?"

"Nope, haven't seen her. I don't know where she is," I said, even though I knew exactly where Gina was lurking.

"Good, that means I can refill." Tommy swiftly removed the Roaring Rucksack with H_2O MegaBoost 2000 that he was wearing on his back.

I was in awe of Tommy's brand-new squirt gun. The huge blaster not only had its own reserve tank, but it also connected to a massive water tank backpack. The Roaring Rucksack with H_2O MegaBoost 2000 was truly a water-soaking technology that was worthy of the new millennium.

Candice and I treaded water as we giddily watched the sitting duck fix his toy. Even Diana stopped sulking about cannonballs to take in the highly anticipated event.

Seconds after Tommy dunked his main tank into the pool, Gina snuck out from behind the cooler, where she had been hiding for the past five minutes.

"Who's the Ruler of Rad and Lord of the Land now!" Gina yelled as she doused her target with water from an identical Roaring Rucksack with H_2O MegaBoost 2000.

"No fair, I'm refilling! You can't do that to me while I'm refilling! You're breaking the rules of engagement!" Tommy shouted. He tried to defend himself with the reserve tank, but it was no match against a fully loaded Roaring Rucksack. "You're gonna get it, Gina!"

"I don't think so!" she squealed before disappearing into the backyard.

Tommy slung the semifilled backpack over his shoulders and took off after Gina. As he rounded a picnic table, he slammed into Bobby, who was walking across the patio. "Outta the way!"

"Watch it!" Bobby yelled after his brother. "You almost made me spill."

I looked at the pitcher and stack of red cups that Bobby was carrying. "Is that your mom's pink lemonade?"

"Freshly made!"

Mrs. McNutt's pink lemonade was famous. She was the only parent who made summer lemonade from scratch, and she made the pink kind every time. I didn't know why pink tasted better than yellow, but it always did. Much like restaurant pizza, pink lemonade just had a certain something special.

Candice, Diana, and I climbed out of the pool at full throttle and accepted cups of ice-cold deliciousness from Bobby.

"Aah," I exclaimed, after downing half a glass. "Hits the spot."

"This is the best," Candice said.

"Thank you, Bobby!" Diana said. She raised the cup to her mouth, then shrieked and threw the drink to the ground.

"Yuck, you spilled all over my foot!" I said.

Diana scrambled onto a chair and struggled to speak. "Sp . . . sp . . . sp . . ."

"What are you doing?" Candice asked, before turning deadly serious. "Did you see a yellow jacket? Where? Where is it?" She spun around, ducking out of the way of possible wasps.

"Sp . . . spiders!" Diana sputtered. She pointed to the lemonade puddle on the pavement. "In the ice!"

With a satisfied cackle, Bobby picked up the only two ice cubes that hadn't melted on contact with the scorching concrete. "Fake spiders inside fake ice cubes. Best ninety-nine cents I've spent all summer at Otter's!"

That statement was high praise for the ice cubes. Especially considering that Bobby had nailed Mrs. Parish in the face with a squirting camera during a celebratory pizza party.

Diana flew off the chair and roared, "It's not funny!"

"It's kinda funny," Candice said, covering a smile with her hand.

"You're right, Diana. It's not funny," Bobby said. "It's *hysterical*!"

"It's not funny," she said. "You wanna know what I think is funny?"

Before Bobby could answer, Diana yelled, "*This* is funny!" and pushed him and his spider ice cubes into the pool.

My jaw dropped the moment that Bobby was airborne. Diana "No Running in the Pool Area" Rodriguez had pushed a McNutt into the water! I never would have believed it had I not seen it with my own two eyes.

"Who's laughing now, Bobby?" Diana taunted.

"Me!" Candice said. She was in stiches and struggled to form words. "I'm laughing so much I think I'm gonna pee."

"But you're not going to P. Tonnes until next week," I said, which made her crack up even more.

Diana, freshly released from being the butt of spider jokes, joined the fun. "That's right, Candice. Next week is when you're going to P. Tonnes."

"Stop, stop, stop!" Candice howled as she collapsed in a fit of belly laughs.

Bobby treaded water and grinned at Diana. "That was awesome! Can you push me in again?"

Just then Johnny rushed into the pool area holding a package. "They arrived! They arrived!"

"Aw, nuts! I dropped my ice cubes!" Bobby cried before sinking into the water to hunt for them.

"My Ace Adventure 500 walkie-talkies arrived in the mail!" Johnny held up his shiny new pair of secret-communications devices. "Long-range edition!"

"Yes!" I said. "Now we can do real stakeouts like real detectives."

"Let's go test them in Scotland Yard and see how far they can reach from the picnic pavilion," Johnny said.

Bobby surfaced, took a huge gulp of air, and resubmerged in search of his ninety-nine-cent treasures from Otter's Joke Shop.

"Move it, people!" Gina barked. She and Tommy, both soaking wet, had returned and were in a wild race to refill their squirt guns.

At the exact same moment, Johnny spotted the pitcher. "Ooh, pink lemonade!" He beelined to the table, nearly colliding with Gina, who had just leaped over the cooler.

"Johnny—I said move it!" She soon realized that he was running to Mrs. McNutt's summer specialty and quickly grabbed Tommy's arm. "Truce! Truce! Pink-lemonade truce!"

Tommy stopped dead in his tracks and took stock of Gina's trustworthiness. "OK, truce. But we both have to take off our Roaring Rucksacks at the same time."

"Deal."

While keeping a watchful eye on each other, Gina and Tommy simultaneously shed their gear and rushed to pour themselves a drink.

Candice, finally recovered from her giggle fit, picked up one of Johnny's new walkie-talkies. "These will be great for the sixth-grade trip to the corn maze. We'll be the first ones to find our way out and win the prize for sure."

"And they'll come in handy on the sixth-grade camping trip next spring," I said.

"It's pretty amazing to think that there wouldn't be any of these trips if it wasn't for us," Diana said.

"Stupid grown-ups and their stupid plan to close FDR," Johnny snickered. "Not when the Sherlock Pines Gang is on the watch!"

"We saved everything," Gina said between gulps of pink lemonade.

"Because we're a team," I said. "Like the McNutts told us, when in the course of human events . . . something, something, something . . . kids have a constitutional right to stop grown-ups who are being unfair and dumb and mean."

Tommy finished chugging from his red cup. "You got it! Couldn't have said it better myself." Then he raucously belched, and his family's beagles began howling three houses away.

Bobby exploded out of the water with a triumphant splash and held his ice cubes in the air. "Found 'em!"

Diana poured herself a spider-free drink and raised it in a toast. "To the Sherlock Pines Gang!"

"To us!" Candice shouted.

"And to graduating high school in one big group, just like the Bayside gang!" Johnny said.

"Woo-hoo!" Bobby slapped the water in applause until he saw that the ice cubes had slipped out of his hands again. "Oh come on!"

"And to being sixth graders at FDR—*together*!" I said.

"Sherlock Pines Gang forever!" we cheered.

I couldn't stop grinning from ear to ear.

Yes, I, Becky Dulles, was truly going to be a Big Kid sixth grader at Franklin D. Roosevelt Elementary, with all the perks and benefits I'd been looking forward to!

I couldn't wait for the first day of school when I could tell my sixth-grade teacher the 100 percent–true tale about what I did on my vacation—the story of how the Sherlock Pines Gang found buried treasure, saved our school, and became friends forever during that summer we stole our permanent records.

ABOUT THE AUTHOR

Kersti Niebruegge graduated from the University of Wisconsin–Madison and has worked for *Conan*, *Late Night with Seth Meyers*, and BBC Worldwide. *That Summer We Stole Our Permanent Records* is her first book for young readers. She is also the author of *The Zonderling* and *Mistake, Wisconsin*.

And even though Kersti hasn't been in school for a very long time, she would still like to know what all those teachers wrote in her permanent record.

www.kerstiniebruegge.com